W9-ANU-096

doppelganger

doppelganger

PETE HAUTMAN
WINNER OF THE NATIONAL BOOK AWARD
AND MARY LOGUE

G. P. Putnam's Sons

G. P. PUTNAM'S SONS
A division of Penguin Young Readers Group.
Published by The Penguin Group.
Penguin Group (USA) Inc., 375 Hudson Street, New York, NY 10014, U.S.A.

Penguin Group (Canada), 90 Eglinton Avenue East, Suite 700, Toronto, Ontario M4P 2Y3, Canada
(a division of Pearson Penguin Canada Inc.).
Penguin Books Ltd, 80 Strand, London WC2R 0RL, England.
Penguin Ireland, 25 St. Stephen's Green, Dublin 2, Ireland (a division of Penguin Books Ltd.).
Penguin Group (Australia), 250 Camberwell Road, Camberwell, Victoria 3124, Australia
(a division of Pearson Australia Group Pty Ltd).
Penguin Books India Pvt Ltd, 11 Community Centre, Panchsheel Park, New Delhi—110 017, India.
Penguin Group (NZ), 67 Apollo Drive, Rosedale, North Shore 0745, Auckland, New Zealand
(a division of Pearson New Zealand Ltd).
Penguin Books (South Africa) (Pty) Ltd, 24 Sturdee Avenue, Rosebank, Johannesburg 2196, South Africa.
Penguin Books Ltd, Registered Offices: 80 Strand, London WC2R 0RL, England.

 Published simultaneously in Canada.
Design by Gina DiMassi. Text set in Granjon.

Library of Congress Cataloging-in-Publication Data
Hautman, Pete, 1952–
Doppelganger / by Pete Hautman and Mary Logue. p. cm. — (The Bloodwater mysteries)
Summary: High school newspaper reporter Roni finds an age-progressed photograph on a
missing children's website of a boy that looks just like her sidekick Brian, throwing the pair into
an investigation of Brian's past and family heritage.
[1. Identity—Fiction. 2. Missing children—Fiction. 3. Adoption—Fiction. 4. Korean Americans—
Fiction. 5. Mystery and detective stories.] I. Logue, Mary. II. Title.
PZ7.H2887Do 2008 [Fic]—dc22 2007020421

ISBN 978-0-399-24379-0
3 5 7 9 10 8 6 4

For Luke and Mary Brindle

contents

doppelganger

1
an article of interest

Brian Bain heard a familiar thump on the side of the house, the sound he had been waiting for. He abandoned his computer in mid-keystroke, ran down the steps and through the living room, and opened the front door. He looked around. The paperboy was already out of sight.

It took him a few seconds to find the source of the thump. Then he saw the newspaper stuck deep in the rosebush next to the steps. Too excited to care about a few small scratches, Brian reached in through the thorny stems and sweet-smelling blossoms and extracted the morning edition of the *Bloodwater Clarion.*

He sat down on the steps and immediately began paging through the paper. A few seconds later, on page twenty-three, he found it.

The photograph took up almost half the page: his own face, almost life-size, smiling and holding up a paper airplane. The caption beneath the photo read, "Brian Bain, 13, displays his winning design in the Zeb Bloodwater Paper-Airplane Contest."

More than half a century ago, Zeb Bloodwater, the

grandson of Bloodwater's founder, had fashioned a pair of wings made from brown paper bags and balsa struts, then launched himself off the two-hundred-foot-high Barn Bluff. The *Clarion*'s annual paper-airplane contest was in memory of Zeb's first—and final—attempt at flight.

This summer, Brian had won the contest, which required that the airplane be folded from the front page of the *Bloodwater Clarion.* He named his airplane the SS-XLR8. First prize was a framed certificate and—most important—his picture in the paper.

Famous again, Brian thought as he admired the photograph. He had been in the paper twice before, but both times it had been with Roni Delicata. First, there had been the article about the Alicia Camden kidnapping a few months ago. He had been in the paper again when he and Roni had uncovered the secret behind the vicious attack on a local archaeologist. But those pictures had been much smaller, and Roni had been standing in front, hogging the camera.

This time Brian was alone on the page, and the picture was huge. Best of all, it had nothing to do with crime solving or Roni Delicata. It was all about him and his accomplishments.

Brian imagined Roni flipping through the paper and then coming upon his face staring out at her. He grinned.

She would be excruciatingly jealous.

Fifty miles away, a woman reading the online edition of the *Bloodwater Clarion* came across Brian's picture. Her heart began to pound. She reached out and ran her fingers across the image of his face.

Softly, so quietly no one else could hear her, she said, "Oh, no. He must not find you. I will try to keep you safe."

Another woman also paused upon seeing Brian Bain's picture. She stared at the photo in disbelief. Her lips stretched across her face in an unfamiliar way. It felt so peculiar she was afraid she had somehow injured her face. Then she realized that she was smiling for the first time in many years.

She picked up her phone and dialed.

Thirty miles southeast of Bloodwater, in a dilapidated mobile home tucked into a wooded coulee, a telephone rang. The man sprawled on the bed opened one bloodshot eye and glared at it. The ringing continued. The man reached over the side of the bed, picked up a muddy boot, and hurled it at the telephone. He missed, but the ringing stopped. Grumbling, the man pulled a blanket over his head and tried to go back to sleep.

A few seconds later, the phone began to ring again. The man cursed and rolled out of bed, dragging the blanket with him, stepped over the sleeping dog, and picked up the receiver.

"What," he said.

"Good news, baby," said the woman on the phone. "I found him."

2

among the missing

Roni Delicata took the fruit bar from its box and closed the freezer door. She tore the paper wrapper at the top, stripping it down as if peeling a banana. Admiring the bright color of the frozen fruit bar—so pink it almost hurt her eyes to look at it—she removed the last of the wrapper and threw it in the trash can beneath the kitchen sink.

"How many of those are you planning to eat?" Nick Delicata's voice stopped Roni's tongue in mid-lick.

Roni looked at the frozen fruit bar in her hand, then at her mother.

"It's made with real strawberries," she said.

"Yes, and real sugar, too," Nick said.

"It's only my second one."

"It's your third one this afternoon. I thought you were on a diet. Last night you hardly ate a bite of my lasagna."

Roni shrugged and took a big bite out of the fruit bar so she wouldn't have to explain why she hadn't been able to eat the gummy, sticky disaster that her mother called lasagna. As for her diet, well . . . that hadn't been going so well. She blamed it on sheer boredom. But she had another six weeks until school started—plenty of time to starve herself.

"You shouldn't eat just because you're bored," Nick said, performing that irritating mind-reading trick that mothers do so well.

"Who says I'm bored?" Roni said.

"I know you. You've got the midsummer blahs. If you're not in the middle of investigating for some article—or solving one of your mysteries—you do nothing but sleep, stare at your computer, and eat junk food."

"I read, too," Roni said.

"Then maybe you'd like to help me with these letters." Roni's mom was the secretary to the mayor of Bloodwater. She often brought work home with her, and that afternoon she had come home with two boxes of letters to the mayor, most of them having to do with Mayor Buddy Berglund's recent proposal to make Bloodwater House his official residence—at the taxpayers' expense. The citizens of Bloodwater were somewhat perturbed. Nick was dividing the letters into three piles: "opposed," "vehemently opposed," and "threatening."

"No, thanks," said Roni, heading for the stairs. "I have to get back to my room. I'm reading the dictionary."

Nick laughed and shook her head.

Roni settled into her desk chair, woke up her computer, and looked upon the face of a girl who had been abducted in

Milwaukee, Wisconsin, several weeks earlier. Vanessa Angel Charleston, age six, believed to be in the company of her mother, Angelina Charleston. Roni studied the girl's face, then read the specifics: height, weight, hair color, eye color, birthmarks, etc. She stared fiercely at the picture until she was sure that if she ever saw Vanessa Charleston, she would immediately recognize her.

She licked her fruit bar just in time to keep it from dripping onto her keyboard, and clicked the next name on the missing-children website. Sooner or later, she would run into one of these lost, abducted, or runaway kids. What a story it would make if one of these kids were found in Bloodwater! Roni dreamed of becoming an investigative reporter. Finding a missing child could be her big break. She imagined her byline, P. Q. Delicata, on the front page of *The New York Times*. At the very least, she could write about it in her column for the *Bloodwater Pump,* the high school newspaper.

Most of the younger missing kids had been snatched by one of their own parents—probably after a nasty divorce. The older ones, including a lot of girls her age—sixteen—were probably runaways. Only a few were victims of stranger abductions.

Roni clicked on the next name. Bryce Doblemun. A cute-looking Asian kid. She licked her fruit bar and scrolled down, reading. Abducted by his adoptive mother at age three years and eleven months—almost ten years ago. She scrolled down to a second image: an "age-progressed" photo of the same kid—an artist had taken the photo of the young

Bryce Doblemun and "aged" it to what he might look like ten years later.

Roni stared at the age-progressed photo.

The boy in the photo stared back at her.

Roni's mouth slowly fell open.

"Impossible," she said.

A large pink strawberry-flavored blob dripped onto her keyboard.

She knew him.

3

a real scar

Brian Bain sat at his desk admiring his picture from the *Bloodwater Clarion,* now pinned up on his bedroom wall. He had decided not to call Roni about it—he would wait for her to stumble across it on her own. He looked at the phone, willing it to ring, and—amazingly—it did.

He checked the caller ID. It was Roni. Perfect.

Brian picked up the phone. "Bain Aviation."

"Brian? It's me. Are you online?"

Brian touched a key on his laptop and the screen came to life.

"Yep. Hey, did you see the paper?"

Roni ignored him. "Go to this site," she said. She gave him the web address.

Brian typed in the address. "Did you see the paper?" he asked again.

"No. Has the site loaded yet?"

"Wait . . . here it is." The missing-kids website popped up.

"Now type 'Bryce Doblemun' into the search box." She spelled out the name.

Brian typed it in and hit the search button. A little kid's photo came up.

"What do you think?" Roni asked.

"About what?"

"Scroll down."

Brian scrolled down to the age-progressed photo.

"Look like anybody you know?" Roni asked.

Brian stared at the face on his computer screen. It looked vaguely familiar. "Not really."

"It's *you*!" Roni said.

"You're crazy," he said. "Look how fat his cheeks are."

"Just like your cheeks," Roni said.

Brian's eyes went from the image on his computer to the article tacked on the wall.

"I do not have fat cheeks. Besides, I'm not missing."

"Yeah, but . . ."

"But what?"

"Well, do you actually remember anything from before you were adopted?"

"I was, like, six months old!"

"Are you sure?"

Brian didn't say anything for several seconds. The question bothered him more than he cared to let on.

"You still there?" Roni asked.

"His eyes are squinty. I do not have squinty eyes."

"You do when you laugh."

Brian decided then and there to give up laughing,

especially when he was around Roni. It wouldn't be easy. Roni could be pretty funny.

"He's older," Brian said.

"You're both thirteen. His birthday's on the twelfth, yours is on the twenty-first. That could just be a typo."

"You think all Asians look the same," he said.

"I do not!"

"How many Asian kids do you know?"

"You mean besides you? Lots."

"Name three."

"Cynthia Lee. Denis Nguyen. Aaron White. And none of them look anything like you."

"Cindy's a girl, and she's from China, Denis is eighteen years old and only half Vietnamese, and Aaron White is Native American."

"What*ever*. Are you still looking at the picture? Look at yourself and compare."

Once again, Brian looked at the photo of himself in the newspaper, then back at the image on his computer screen.

"He does look Korean. But his ears are different."

"Not *that* different. And what about his name?"

Brian looked again at the missing kid's name. Bryce Doblemun. "What about it?"

"*Bryce? Brian?* Pretty close, don't you think?"

"I'll tell you what I think," he said. "I think you're insane."

"Yeah, well, maybe I'm crazy enough to call the missing-kids hotline and tell them I've found Bryce Doblemun."

Brian felt his insides lurch. How come every time he talked to Roni, everything got so scary and complicated?

"Don't," he said.

"Why not?"

"Because . . . because I need a donut."

Roni laughed. "*Now* you're speaking my language!"

"Bratten's Bakery? Twenty minutes?"

"I'm on my way."

Was there really a resemblance?

Brian stared at the face on his computer screen. Bryce Doblemun's image swam in and out of focus. One moment he felt as if he was looking into a crazy mirror, a second later it was like staring at a complete stranger.

Maybe they were somehow related. Brian's parents had told him that his South Korean mother had given him up for adoption when he was just a few months old. He might have cousins, or even a brother or sister. He would probably never know. His biological relatives were six thousand miles away in a country he did not remember. The weird thing was, when he tried to recall his distant past, sometimes he thought he remembered living with another family when he was little—a few faint glimpses of a previous life: A big man who laughed a lot. A little dog. A lady with red hair.

He scrolled up to the photo of Vera Doblemun, the boy's adoptive mother. She was a thin, pinched-looking woman with light hair. The photo was black-and-white, and the description did not include her hair color. Her face did not look at all familiar.

According to the website, Bryce and Vera Doblemun had disappeared from their home in Minneapolis. Roni would probably make a big deal out of the fact that Minneapolis was less than an hour away from Bloodwater. Roni could make a big deal out of oatmeal.

Brian closed his eyes. He thought he remembered a little curly-haired dog with a pointy nose, and a swing set. The memories were faint and disconnected, like a dream. He had always assumed that they *were* dreams—like the time he remembered Bugs Bunny visiting him in his bedroom.

How could he tell what was real and what wasn't?

He remembered running on a sidewalk with the little dog, and tripping and hurting his elbow.

Brian looked at the old white scar on his elbow. That, at least, was real.

4

the rhododendron incident

Bruce Bain stood atop a rickety stool in his crowded, book-crammed study, trying to read the spines of the books that lined a sagging shelf just below the ceiling.

"Hey, Dad," Brian said.

Bruce Bain flinched, but managed to retain his balance.

"One moment, son," he said. "You haven't seen my copy of *Somatic Empathy in Nematode Neurons,* have you?"

"Uh, not lately. Hey, did we used to have a dog?"

"A dog? Why do you ask?"

"I remember a dog," Brian said.

"I'm allergic to dogs, son."

"So . . . did you and Mom adopt me, or did you abduct me?"

"You'll have to ask your mother, son. She keeps all the family records."

Brian rolled his eyes. His father, absorbed in his own little world, had heard Brian's words, but hadn't really listened to what he was saying.

"Aha!" said Mr. Bain. "Here's my copy of *Sea Snail Aquaculture Techniques*! I've been looking all over for that!"

"I'm going out," Brian said. "If Mom comes home, tell her I've gone out to get my eyeball pierced."

"I'll let her know."

Brian stopped his skateboard at the top of Grant Street and looked down the block-long hill. It was not the steepest hill in town, but he could get going about fifteen miles an hour by the time he reached the intersection with Third Street. On a skateboard, that was *fast.* The trick was to make a split-second decision in the final twenty feet before hitting the cross street, when approaching cars—if there were any—became visible. He would have about a tenth of a second to either go for the crossing or bail out into Mrs. Atkinson's rhododendron bush. Brian had rolled down the hill lots of times before. So far he hadn't had to bail out once.

He was standing with one foot on his skateboard getting himself psyched up when a small green Hyundai pulled up beside him. The driver was an Asian woman, maybe thirty years old. He had never seen her around town before, and he usually noticed people of Asian ancestry, since there were hardly any in Bloodwater. And this woman looked like she could be Korean.

She lowered her window. "You aren't planning to go down that hill on your skateboard, are you?" she asked. She had a strong accent. Definitely Korean.

Brian shook his head.

"Good," she said. She added something that sounded like a garbled version of the word *choosing.* Their eyes locked, and for a moment Brian felt as if his chest were full of ginger ale.

She could be my real mother, he thought.

She smiled and nodded. The moment passed. Brian watched her drive down the hill and turn left.

What had she said? Brian replayed the strange word in his head, trying to remember if it was something he had learned at the Korean language camp he had attended last summer. Choo-Sing? Cho-Sun?

Suddenly he had it: *Cho-sim*. He knew that word. It *was* Korean, and he remembered what it meant.

Beware!

Beware of what?

Brian shook his head. This was all Roni's fault. Every time anything unexplained happened, she assumed it meant something dreadful and mysterious. And now, thanks to her, every time he saw a Korean woman, he would wonder if she was his biological mother.

He looked down the hill and narrowed his eyes. Beware? Ha! He'd done this lots of times before.

He pushed off.

Bratten's Café and Bakery, in downtown Bloodwater, was home to the best donuts in the county. It was also, as Roni had discovered a few weeks earlier, a Wi-Fi hot spot. On most days she could pick up a strong, unsecured wireless signal from one of the tenants who lived above the coffee shop. Roni was sitting at one of the outdoor tables with her laptop, looking at the picture of Bryce Doblemun, when she heard the clatter of a skateboard. Brian rolled up to the table and kicked up his board. He had red scratches all over his arms and face, and his T-shirt was torn.

"What happened to you?" she asked.

"Got in a fight with a rhododendron bush," Brian said. He took a newspaper from under his arm and plunked it on the table. "Where's your Vespa?"

"Good old Hillary has a flat tire. She's at Darwin Dipstick's garage. Why were you fighting with a bush?"

"Don't ask."

"*You're* in a mood. Better get yourself a donut." Roni had already finished her raspberry-stuffed long john.

Brian pointed at the newspaper. "Page twenty-three," he said.

Roni read the article about Brian's paper-airplane triumph while Brian browsed the pastry counter. He returned to the table with a chocolate-covered cake donut—her third-favorite. When he sat down across from her, she stared at him as if she'd never seen him before. He looked different, somehow more exotic now.

Brian took a bite out of his donut, chewed for a moment, then noticed her staring at him. "Why are you looking at me that way?" he asked.

"I've never met an abducted adoptee airplane builder before."

"Very funny." He set his donut back on the paper plate.

Roni had never seen Brian take more than thirty seconds to devour a pastry. "I think my dad's losing it," he said.

"You've been saying that ever since I've known you."

"I told him I was getting my eyeball pierced. I think he believed me."

"Do you ever wonder about your real parents?"

"Real? You mean like not imaginary?"

"I mean *biological*."

Brian shrugged. "Oh. Not really. When I think about it, which isn't often, it's more like a science fiction story, like I came from a different planet. Planet Korea."

"I always suspected you were an alien." She turned her computer so the screen faced Brian. "You think he's from the same planet?"

"I don't know, but he's not me. I mean, even if I did live with another adoptive family when I was little, I don't think my name was Doblemun, and"—he pointed at the picture of Vera Doblemun—"I don't remember *her* at all."

"Wait—you lived with another family?"

"I remember some stuff. But it was probably a dream. How much do *you* remember from when you were four?"

"Lots," Roni said. But when she thought about it, she wasn't all that sure.

"My parents did not abduct me," Brian said.

"True, they don't seem like the kidnapping type," Roni said.

"I asked my dad about it."

Roni laughed. "You asked your dad if he abducted you?"

"Yeah. He said I should ask my mom."

"If she abducted you, do you think she'd admit it?"

"Look, this whole thing is stupid." Brian stood up. "My parents would not lie to me. This is just some kid who, just because he's my age and Asian, you think looks like me. Which he doesn't."

Roni looked down at Brian's donut. "Are you going to finish that?"

"I'm not hungry."

Roni didn't wait for him to change his mind. She took a bite, claiming it as hers. So much for her one-pastry-a-week diet.

Brian said, "I'm sure my mom knows all about this kid. It happened here in Minnesota, and a kid getting abducted is a big deal, right?"

"Not so much if he gets snatched by one of his own parents."

"Anyway, I'm sure she knows about it. I mean, it's her job."

"So are you gonna ask her?"

Brian shrugged.

"Where is she?"

"At the police station."

5

a family matter

Brian sailed into the police department, waved at Agnes, who was behind the counter, and got his head rubbed by George Firth, one of the old-timers with the Bloodwater Police. He circled past the entrance to the jail and down the hall toward his mother's office. Roni stayed close behind him. Brian loved these rare moments when he was the one in charge. Usually, he was trying to keep up with Roni, but the police station was his territory. He'd been coming here for as long as he could remember.

Detective Annette Bain was digging through a file cabinet and talking to herself. He heard her say something that sounded like, "Drat barn wigglesnoot trashooper!"

Sometimes she could be almost as weird as his father.

"Hi, Mom," he said.

Mrs. Bain shot a look at Brian, and then at Roni, then back at Brian. She stood up straight and asked, "What happened to you?"

"Nothing," said Brian.

"You look like you've been in a fight with a bobcat."

"Oh." Brian remembered that he was a little scratched up. "Actually, it was a rhododendron."

"And what were you . . . oh, never mind. Have you come to lodge a complaint against the bush?"

"Um, it wasn't really the bush's fault."

Mrs. Bain pulled a file from the cabinet. "Hello, Roni. Are you the one who caused my son to engage in fisticuffs with a rhododendron?"

Detective Annette Bain did not entirely approve of Roni Delicata. Brian could hardly blame her. Every time he nearly got himself killed, it seemed Roni was somehow involved.

"I have an alibi," said Roni.

"Show her the picture," Brian said.

Roni, for once, just did what he asked her to do. She opened her laptop and turned it on. A few seconds later the age-progressed image of Bryce Doblemun was looking out at them.

His mom sat down behind her desk and stared at the slightly chunky Korean boy's face. "I hadn't seen this latest age progression," she said.

"You *know* about him?" Roni asked.

"Bryce Doblemun? Of course I do. He disappeared several years ago from his home in Minneapolis along with his adoptive mother. Apparently she ran off with him. There was quite an investigation. As far as I know, they are both still missing." She frowned at Brian, then at Roni. "Why are you showing me this?"

"Roni thinks he looks like me."

"Ah, I see. Looking for another mystery, Roni?"

"You have to admit, it is kind of a coincidence," Roni said. "He looks just like Brian. Same age. And he disappeared from Minneapolis, which is pretty close to Bloodwater. Also, he's an adoptee."

Mrs. Bain raised one eyebrow. Brian knew that raised eyebrow well. Roni was treading on dangerous ground.

"And?" said Mrs. Bain.

Roni, to Brian's horror and admiration, plowed ahead.

"So . . . how did you get Brian?" she asked.

Mrs. Bain sat back in her chair and placed one finger on the side of her chin. "We adopted him, as you well know."

"How old was he?"

"Roni, I understand your curiosity, but don't you think that this is rather personal?"

"I was just—"

"Really, Roni, it's a family matter." She stood up. "Now, if you two sleuths will excuse me, I have work to do."

Brian knew that if he didn't say something, Roni would never let him forget it.

"Mom, do you have, um, papers for me? Adoption papers?"

"Of course we do." She looked at her watch. "Can we talk about this later, sweetie?"

His mom called him "sweetie" only when she was trying not to be mad at him.

Mrs. Bain picked up the file on her desk. "I'll see you at dinner," she said. "And when you get home, put some antiseptic on those scratches." She walked out of the room.

"I think she knows something she's not telling," Roni said as she shut down her computer.

Brian had a prickly feeling deep in his gut. He was afraid that Roni might be right.

6

the lost emperor

Roni was talking a million miles an hour as they left the courthouse.

". . . and even if your folks really adopted you like they say, maybe Vera Doblemun stole you and then you escaped and got found on a street someplace and you were re-re-orphaned—"

"I don't think there's such a thing as *re*-re-orphaned," Brian said.

"Whatever—you know what I mean. Or maybe Vera Doblemun was horribly murdered by a gang of child stealers and they sold you to an adoption agency. We should find out which agency you got adopted from. We could break in and look through their records. We could—"

Brian stopped. Roni kept walking. It took her a couple of seconds to realize she'd left Brian behind.

"What?" she said, looking back.

"I don't want you stirring things up," Brian said.

Roni looked at him as if he were insane. "You don't want me to investigate? We need to find out—"

"Shut *up*! I *know* who I am. My parents are not criminals."

"I just—"

"Suppose you found out that your mom maybe wasn't really your mom. Would you want me running all over town dredging up your family history?"

"I wouldn't turn down your help."

"I'm not saying I don't want your help. I just want to find things out my way, at least to start."

Looking chastened, Roni said, "Will you tell me what she says, at least?"

"Absolutely." Brian dropped his skateboard to the sidewalk and caught it with his foot. "If I find out I'm really the Lost Emperor of Korea, you'll be the first to know."

As Roni watched the Lost Emperor of Korea roll off, she was already thinking of ways to move the investigation along. Don't go stirring things up? Who did he think he was dealing with? Stirring things up was her specialty.

She slung her backpack over her shoulders and shoved her hands into the pockets of her jeans—sort of a boy thing to do, but it seemed to help her think. Besides, she had decided not to care what anybody thought of her. That Roni Delicata, she just does her own thing, people would say. Problem was, nobody seemed to notice.

She looked around to see if anybody was noticing now.

Downtown Bloodwater on a weekday afternoon was not exactly a happening place, unless you were a sixty-something retired schoolteacher in the market for some moldy old antiques. Roni saw several of that breed carrying large shopping bags and peering into shop windows. To them, she was all but invisible—just another slightly schlumpy, slightly overweight, slightly loitering teenager. The only kids her age they really noticed were the big scary ones.

Sooner or later, she thought, they'll notice me. One big case was all it would take—a missing kid found, the capture of a dangerous criminal, or a story on the front page of the paper. The day I graduate from high school, she decided, I'm out of here. She would go to London, Paris, New York . . . even Minneapolis would do. Someplace where things were happening, where she would fit in with the other strange people who just did what they felt like doing.

Until then, she would keep digging up information about the missing Bryce Doblemun—even if Brian Bain didn't approve.

Real emperors had thrones, crowns, and loyal subjects. It sounded like a lot of work. Were there ever emperors in Korea? Had Korea ever lost an emperor? He would have to look it up.

As he walked into the quiet house, Brian did not feel like royalty. He felt like a vague, amorphous blob that was slowly floating around the world, twirling in all directions, tethered to no place at all. Yikes. If he didn't watch it, the next thing he knew, he'd be writing poetry.

Brian heard his father muttering to himself in his office, but he didn't feel like trying to get his attention. Way too much work. He walked quietly up the stairs, collapsed on his bed, and stared at the ceiling. What was his earliest memory? The little dog? The red-haired lady? They seemed like a dream, and maybe they were. But what about his earliest memories of his current parents? His mom liked to tell a story about taking Brian to the county fair and letting him wander. He had walked around without ever once looking back to see where his parents were. Of course, they'd been right behind him all the time, following him to make sure he didn't get into trouble.

Brian remembered that day, or at least he thought he did. The way he remembered it, he had been searching for his little dog.

His mom—his second or third mom, he should probably call her, maybe even shorten it to Mom^3—thought it was a funny story because he had been such an independent and fearless kid. "You just took off on your own," she would say with a laugh. "If we hadn't stopped you, you'd have joined the carnival!"

What else did he remember? Going on a ride. Riding on a big duck that went around in circles with a lot of other big ducks. A kiddie ride, but it had been exciting at the time. Seeing his parents' blurred faces watching him as he went around and around and around.

Brian felt as if he were melting into his bed. If he didn't know who he really was, was he in danger of dissolving? He rolled off the bed and fell to the floor on his hands and knees. He crawled to his dresser, pulled open the bottom drawer, and dug into the far corner under a sweater he hardly ever wore because it made his neck itch. He pulled out a small wooden box and removed a small metal coin. On one side was a picture of a building surrounded by Korean writing. The other side had a big numeral 10 next to the words THE BANK OF KOREA 1972. It was the only thing he had from Korea, and he couldn't even remember where he had gotten it.

He thought of biting it to see if it was gold. It had a goldish glint to it. He wondered what it was worth—maybe he should take it on *Antiques Roadshow*. Tell his story. Maybe his country would discover him then.

Maybe he really was a lost emperor.

7
darwin dipstick

Batman has his Batmobile; Green Lantern has his ring; Wonder Woman has her invisible airplane. Roni needed Hillary, her trusty Vespa, if she was going to seriously work on this case. Roni had run over another nail, and Darwin Depaul—better known as Darwin Dipstick—had said he could fix the Vespa in a jiffy. A "jiffy" meant she needed to stay on his case if she wanted Hillary back before the snow flew.

She decided not to phone Darwin. Instead, she would drop in on him at his gas station. Sometimes it was best to take people by surprise.

When she got to the station, she spotted Hillary in a back corner of the garage, still with the flat front tire. Darwin was sitting behind the cash register reading *Monster Trucks Monthly.*

"Hey, kid," he said, like, *Go away and do not interrupt my important reading.*

"Hey," Roni said back, like, *I'm here, and I'm staying here until I get what I want.*

Darwin sighed, closed his magazine, and ran his grease-blackened fingers through his nonexistent hair, leaving four dark streaks on his bald dome. "Bad news, kid. Your new tire's not in yet."

"I thought you were going to fix the old one."

"That tire of yours has got one too many patches. Had to order you a new one."

"How long is that going to take?"

"Dunno. A couple days?"

Roni took a deep breath to calm herself. Two more days without Hillary? Unthinkable!

"How about you patch the old one anyway," she said.

"Not safe," Darwin said, shaking his head. "That baby blows and you go skidding down the street on your keister, your mama will have my head."

"Yeah, well, if you don't fix it, I'll see that my mom mentions your little junkyard to the mayor again."

Darwin's eyes bugged out. The half acre behind the station was a notorious weed-choked field of automotive scrap. Once every year or two, the mayor's office received a complaint and Darwin was forced to cut the weeds back and organize his rusting treasures in neat rows, a task he despised.

"You wouldn't," he said.

"I would," Roni said.

Darwin's shoulders sagged.

Roni said, "I'll just ride it around town, Darwin. When the new tire comes in, I'll come back and you can replace it."

Defeated, Darwin unfolded his lanky body and stood up. "Okay, but keep it under twenty-five miles an hour."

"I promise." It was all Roni could do to suppress a smile. "Patch her up and I'll get out of your hair." The out-of-your-hair part was a little cruel, seeing as how Darwin had only two tufts of hair on his head, one above each ear.

"This is extortion, you know," said Darwin as they walked back into the service bay.

"Technically, it's blackmail," Roni said.

"That don't make it any better," he said as he grabbed a wrench. He began to remove Hillary's front wheel.

"A girl does what she has to," Roni said.

Darwin snorted. Roni tried not to laugh.

"So I guess that boyfriend of yours is pretty famous now," Darwin said.

"What boyfriend?"

"That Chinese kid you hang around with? I've seen you at the Dairy Queen together."

"He's not my boyfriend. What do you mean, *famous*?"

"Just saw his picture in the paper for that contest."

"I wouldn't call that *famous,*" Roni said.

"Those Chinese are real smart at folding paper," Darwin said.

"You're thinking of the Japanese," Roni said. "They're known for their origami. That's paper folding. Anyway, Brian isn't Chinese. He's Korean, and he was adopted. He's as American as you or me."

"Nope. If he was born outside the country, he can't be president."

"Unlike you?"

Darwin laughed. "I could've run this country easy. If I'd finished high school."

Roni tried to imagine Darwin in the White House. Oddly enough, it wasn't that hard to do.

"Must be weird being a Korean here in Bloodwater," Darwin said as he cleaned the inside of the tire, getting it ready for the patch.

Roni had never really thought how Brian might feel about that. He was just Brian to her. She hardly ever thought about him being from another country.

Darwin said, "This lady stopped in this morning and showed me the picture of him in the paper. Asked me where he lived. Course, I had no idea."

"Who was she?"

"Never seen her before."

"What did she look like?"

"Big." He pressed the new patch into place. "Big and old and scary, with hair like Bozo the Clown."

"Who's Bozo the Clown?" Roni asked.

"Dude with orange hair. Before your time."

Brian lay on his back and balanced the Korean coin on his nose. He heard his mother's car pull into the driveway.

He decided to give her some time to relax. He had found that if he tried to talk to his mother too soon after she got home from work, she often snapped at him. Almost as if she were talking to a criminal suspect and not her own darling son.

After a few minutes, he got up and put the coin back in its box. He walked down the stairs and went right to the kitchen cabinets to get out the dinner plates. Then he went into the dining room and set the table. He knew how to get on his mom's good side. His mother, sitting in the living room sorting through the mail, watched him through the doorway.

"Thank you, Brian." She walked over and kissed him on the forehead. "What was all that about today? You and Miss Energizer Bunny."

"Roni, you mean?"

"Who else?"

"We were just wondering how you adopted me. Like, how old was I?"

"Brian . . . " She put her finger under his chin and made him look her in the eyes. "You are not that boy in the picture. Roni has a vivid imagination."

"He *does* kind of look like me."

"Who looks like you?" asked Brian's dad, who had just walked into the room.

"Brian and Roni found an age-progressed picture of the Doblemun boy online," explained Mrs. Bain. "They noticed a resemblance."

Mr. Bain furrowed his brow. "Doblemun boy?"

"You remember, dear. The Korean boy who disappeared with his mother a few years back. Up in Minneapolis."

"Oh, yes, I remember now. He did look a bit like Brian." He smiled at Brian. "Maybe you have a doppelganger."

"I feel fine," Brian said.

His father laughed. "A doppelganger is a double, son. Someone who looks exactly like you." His look became thoughtful, almost dreamy. "It has been postulated that everyone has one."

Brian thought for a moment.

"That's kind of creepy," he said.

"There are more than six billion people in the world. Statistically, just about everybody should have a doppelganger someplace."

"In any case," said Mrs. Bain, "you are our one and only son, and we love you."

"So you didn't steal me?"

His parents both laughed, and Brian laughed, too, wondering how he could have thought for a moment that he was somebody else. It wasn't until after dinner, alone in his room, that he realized his mother hadn't answered his question.

8
ms. perhaps

Nick Delicata examined the image on Roni's computer.

"It does look like him," she admitted. "Quite a coincidence."

"Why does it have to be a coincidence?" Roni asked. She and her mother were sitting on their front porch eating dessert: a tray of Oreo cookies. Roni had promised herself she would eat only three. She was on number six.

"Why would you think it was anything *other* than a coincidence?" Nick asked.

"Because Bryce Doblemun was never found. Because Brian doesn't remember when he came to Bloodwater. And he *thinks* he remembers living with a different family when he was really little. And his mom is being all, like, weird about it."

"That's ridiculous, Roni! Why, I remember when the Bains adopted Brian."

"You do?"

"Certainly. Annie Bain was just starting out as a rookie police officer—I was there when the mayor swore her in. She and her husband adopted Brian a few months later."

"When was that?"

"You would have been six or seven years old."

"Which would make Brian three or four! His mom told him he was adopted from Korea when he was a baby! She lied!"

Nick looked startled. "I'm sure you or Brian must have misunderstood. Brian was walking and talking when the Bains adopted him."

"Or *stole* him," Roni said.

Nick laughed. "Roni, that's absurd. Bruce and Annie Bain are not kidnappers."

"Mom, don't you ever read the papers? Every time the cops arrest some guy for some unspeakable crime, the creep's friends and neighbors all say, 'I can't believe it! He seemed like such a nice, quiet man.' I mean, the Bains could be serial killers and we'd never know it."

Nick laughed again, but it wasn't a very good laugh.

"I wonder how we could find out what really happened," Roni said, taking another cookie.

Nick slid the remaining cookies back into the bag and sealed it. "I'm sure there's a reasonable explanation for everything, Roni. In any case, it's between Brian and his parents. Don't stir things up."

"That's what Brian said," Roni muttered.

"You should listen to your friend."

"You don't know me very well, do you?" Roni said.

"I'm afraid I do." Nick stood up. "Give me a hand cleaning up?"

Roni groaned, but picked up the empty milk glasses and followed her mother into the kitchen, where she attacked the dinner dishes with uncharacteristic vigor.

"What's your hurry?" Nick asked.

"I have to get to the library," Roni said.

Doblemun was not a common name. There were no Doblemuns in the Bloodwater phone directory. There were no Doblemuns in the Minneapolis directory, either, or any of the other Minnesota directories on the library shelves. Maybe the Doblemun family—what was left of it—had moved. Roni searched the Internet for Doblemun, but got only three hits: the missing-kids site, a plumbing supply store in Nova Scotia, and the football coach at a Utah high school. Roni reread the information on the missing-kids site.

> Bryce's photo is shown age-progressed to 13 years. He may be in the company of his adoptive mother, Vera Kay Doblemun, who disappeared the same day. They may have left the Minneapolis/St. Paul area. The child's nickname is Bry. Vera Doblemun wears a wig, and may have any hair color. She may use the nickname V.K., or her maiden name, Vera Elizabeth Kay. She has a tattoo of a rose on her left buttock.

Great, Roni thought. Now all I have to do is ask every woman with a wig to show me her butt.

Information. She needed more information, so she went to the information desk. Ms. Paige had helped her out before. Sometimes talking to a librarian is the next best thing to hiring a private detective.

"Ms. Delicata," said Ms. Paige, looking over the tops of her reading glasses. "Solving another mystery?"

Ms. Paige was in her forties, and her hair was the same peculiar shade of yellow as the frames of her eyeglasses. Was she wearing a wig? Possibly.

Roni asked, "Do you have any tattoos?"

"I do not," said Ms. Paige. "Do you?"

"Not yet."

"I would suggest something small. Very small. A semicolon, perhaps. In some out-of-the-way location. Behind your ear, perhaps."

Ms. Paige had a very dry sense of humor, and she loved to use the word *perhaps*.

"*Perhaps* you could help me find someone," Roni said.

"Perhaps," said Ms. Paige.

"I'm looking for a man named Doblemun." She spelled it out. "I don't know his first name. He used to live in Minneapolis."

"You've tried the phone book?"

Roni nodded.

"You've looked online?"

"Yep."

"Do you have any other information?"

Roni told her about Bryce Doblemun disappearing. "I'm trying to locate his father, or some other relative."

"Perhaps you could check the newspaper archives? There must have been some news articles about the abduction. You could probably find the father's first name, at least."

Roni could have kicked herself. Of course!

"Excuse me!" A woman with a voice like a foghorn had come up behind Roni. "Will you be long, young lady?" The woman was quite large, almost a foot taller than Roni and twice as big around. She had metallic blue eyes and a slash of orange lipstick that matched her hair. Two thin, black, arched eyebrows were painted on her forehead about an inch higher than they should have been.

"I require some information," the woman said, pointing at the INFORMATION sign above Ms. Paige's desk.

"I'll be with you in a moment, ma'am," said Ms. Paige in a pointedly quiet voice.

The woman made a *phhht* sound with her lips and crossed her arms over her formidable bosom.

Ms. Paige said to Roni, "You could find the articles if you visited the *Star Tribune* offices up in Minneapolis, or the Minnesota Historical Society in St. Paul. You might even be able to access the archives online, for a few dollars."

"But not for free?"

Ms. Paige smiled. "I'm afraid not."

Behind her, Roni could hear the air whistling in and out of the waiting woman's nostrils.

"I'm not sure I'm ready to spend money on this," Roni said. After paying Darwin for fixing Hillary's flat tire, her cash reserves were getting low.

"There *is* one other possibility," said Ms. Paige. "We have some older phone books in the back." She looked up at the woman waiting behind Roni. "I'll only be a moment." She stood up and walked quickly toward the back of the library. Roni turned to get another look at the rude woman with the whistling nostrils.

"I'm sure she won't be long," Roni said, wondering if this could be the same orange-haired woman who had asked Darwin Dipstick about Brian.

"Hmph," said the woman. "I, for one, do not have time to stand here waiting!" With that, she turned and marched out of the library.

9

suds science

Brian's parents wouldn't outright lie to him. At least he didn't *think* they would.

The challenge was to ask the right questions. Pin them down so they *had* to tell him the truth. The question was, what were the right questions?

Maybe this was one of those skateboard situations—think about it too hard, you lose the guts to try. He opened his bedroom door and listened. He could hear their voices, very faint, maybe coming from the basement. What were they doing in the basement?

Maybe they're talking about me, he thought.

In stocking feet, he walked quietly down the stairs, staying close to the edge to avoid creaks, then slide-walked to the kitchen and stopped at the door to the basement.

"It seemed like a good idea at the time," he heard his dad say.

Brian crept down the stairs, stopping halfway.

"You weren't here," his dad said. "I had to make a decision."

"Not one of your better decisions," Mrs. Bain said. "Now we've got a real mess on our hands."

His dad said something Brian couldn't quite hear. He eased himself down a few more steps.

His mother said, "Brian's not going to be happy about this."

Just then, the telephone rang. Brian tried to run quickly and quietly up the steps so that they wouldn't catch him eavesdropping, but his stocking feet slipped and he slid—thump, thump, thump—down the stairs, landing on his butt at the bottom.

His mother was there in an instant, staring down at him.

"Brian! Are you okay? What happened?"

"The phone is ringing," said Brian.

"Never mind that—are you hurt?"

"I slipped. I'm okay." He sat up.

"What have I told you about running around in your socks!"

"Mom . . . aren't you going to answer the phone?"

"Let the machine get it."

Brian climbed to his feet, then noticed his father standing in the doorway to the laundry room. His pants were wet up to his knees.

"Why are you all wet?" Brian asked.

His dad shrugged. "A little experiment gone awry," he said.

"I asked your father to run a load of wash, and he thought perhaps tripling—"

"Quadrupling," Mr. Bain corrected her.

"*Quadrupling* the amount of detergent might improve our washing machine's performance."

Brian looked through the door into the laundry room. It was two feet deep in suds.

"That's a lot of bubbles," he said. He noticed a pale gray T-shirt in his father's hand. It looked familiar—but different. "Is that . . . ?"

His father held up the gray shirt. Printed across the front was a picture of Albert Einstein. Brian couldn't believe it.

"Not Albert!" he said. "You turned my favorite black T-shirt *gray*?"

"I'm sorry, son," Mr. Bain said. "The dyes apparently could not withstand the enhanced detergent action." He smiled ruefully. "It is, however, very, very clean."

10

albert e.

Divide and conquer.

Who had said that? Julius Caesar? Moses? The Lost Emperor of Korea?

Whoever it was, they must have known something about being a teenager with two parents. Brian knew better than to try to pin them down as a team. He had to get one of them alone, then ask his questions. But at the moment, they were both fighting the Battle of the Suds.

Brian, the emperor of nothing, sat on the stairs, watching them beat back the invasion of the suds monster.

"Isn't it ironic," observed his father, "that one of the hardest things to clean up is soap?"

Brian's mom, attempting to mop the mass of suds that had gathered beneath the laundry tub, did not reply. This was not the first time she had cleaned up after one of her husband's failed experiments.

His dad, who for once was not entirely oblivious, said, "Why don't you relax, dear? I'll clean this up."

Mrs. Bain stood up. "Only if you promise not to apply any of your experimental techniques to the process."

"I promise."

"Then I'll go check the answering machine and see who called." Mrs. Bain went back upstairs, winking at Brian as she passed. "Keep an eye on him," she said.

As soon as she was out of earshot, Brian said, "Dad? Do you remember the first day you brought me home?"

"Of course I do!"

"Tell me about it." Brian walked to the edge of the suds and grabbed his faded Einstein T-shirt from where his dad had hung it.

"Not much to tell, son."

Brian stripped off his shirt and put on Albert Einstein, still wet, just to see if it still fit. He liked the way it clung to his skin.

"Was I crying, or happy, or what?"

"You were a very curious child, into everything, I recall. I'd say you explored the entire house the first hour you were here."

Brian felt his heart starting to pound. If he had been only six months old, he could hardly have "explored the entire house." His next question would be critical—he was afraid that if he said the wrong thing, his dad would clam up and seek reinforcements.

Mr. Bain wrung out the mop. "I wonder if it would be easier to bring in the garden hose from outside and simply spray all these suds into the floor drain."

"Mom said no experiments," Brian said.

His father sighed and went back to mopping the floor.

Brian said, "What ever happened to my dog?"

His dad, distracted by a particularly stubborn mound of suds, said, "Oh. We couldn't take him. Sniffer went to live with another family."

Sniffer! Brian remembered the little brown dog's name now. Now he had proof that his parents had been lying to him all these years. He *had* once lived with another family—the red-haired woman, the laughing man, and Sniffer. And his father had said they couldn't "take" Sniffer. Did that mean they had "taken" Brian? As in *abducted*?

He said, "Dad . . ."

From the top of the stairs, his mom interrupted him. "Brian, could you come up here, please?"

Brian ran up the steps and followed his mom into the kitchen.

"Your father and I have noticed that you've been curious about your ancestry," she began, "and we—"

"Not so much my ancestry," Brian interrupted her. "I was wondering about when you adopted me."

Mrs. Bain sat down at the counter.

"I overheard your father tell you about Sniffer," she said.

"I remember a red-haired lady."

Mrs. Bain nodded. "It's complicated, sweetie. Your father and I planned to tell you everything about your early life, but we've been waiting until you got a little older."

"I'm old enough."

"Perhaps," she said, not meeting his eyes. "You were asking earlier about Bryce Doblemun. You know, every time I see an Asian boy about your age, I wonder if he might be the missing Doblemun boy."

"Roni thinks *I'm* him."

Mrs. Bain smiled, shaking her head. "That girl is quite the drama queen. Oh, by the way, that was her on the phone. Apparently, she is on her way over here to deliver some earth-shattering news."

"That's the only kind of news Roni knows."

His mom laughed, then gave Brian a scarily serious look. "Since you seem so interested in exploring your roots, you should really enjoy your Korean Culture class. Don't forget, it starts tomorrow."

"Tomorrow?" Brian looked at her with a horrified expression. His mother had signed him up for the class ages ago. He had forgotten all about it.

"Don't give me that look," his mother said. "This is the perfect opportunity for you to learn more about the country where you were born. You liked that Korean language camp you went to last summer—"

"Mom, *nobody* likes Korean camp!" Brian had hated it. Not only was it hard work, but the kids with Korean parents had treated the kids with non-Korean parents like some sort of lesser subspecies.

"Maybe it wasn't all fun and games," Mrs. Bain said, "but you learned a lot. You told me you were glad you went."

"I was glad to be done with it, that's for sure."

"In any case, the class begins tomorrow, up in St. Paul. It's on the same days your dad has his Mensa meetings, so he can drive you up and back."

"Okay, but—" Brian heard the familiar putter of Roni's Vespa outside the house.

"That sounds like the bearer of earth-shattering news," said Mrs. Bain.

Roni didn't often come over to his house. She preferred meeting him someplace away from his mother. He had once tried to tell Roni that his mother was not that scary and that Mrs. Bain probably actually liked her. Then he made the big mistake of telling Roni that she and his mother had a lot in common. That explosion was bigger than any chemical reaction he had ever set off.

As Roni walked up the front steps, she looked at his wet shirt and asked, "What happened to Albert E.?" Roni had an eagle eye. Just like his mom.

"My dad did the laundry." Brian sat down on the steps and she joined him.

"Did your dad forget to use the dryer?"

"I wanted to rescue the shirt before he did any more damage. Besides, it feels good wet. What's up?"

"I found out where Bryce Doblemun lived in Minneapolis. I went to the library and Ms. Paige helped me. It was genius. They had some old phone books in storage, and we found the address in one that was ten years old—before Bryce Doblemun disappeared—a listing for Lawrence and

Vera Doblemun." Her voice fell. "Unfortunately, the number's disconnected."

"I thought you were going to drop the case," Brian said.

"How long have you known me?"

"Actually, not all that long," Brian said. "But long enough."

"Did you talk to your parents?"

"Yeah, but I didn't find out much. Except that I wasn't a baby when they adopted me."

"See!" Roni punched him in the shoulder. "I told you! According to my mom, you were three or four when you were adopted."

"Ouch. You *told* me I was *abducted.* Just because I was adopted later than I thought doesn't mean I got snatched."

"It doesn't mean you weren't, either. Which indicates that you might have been."

Brian could not always follow Roni's unique interpretation of the rules of logic.

"I used to have a dog named Sniffer," he said.

Roni didn't seem to be listening. "Look, we need information. I'm going to drive up to the Doblemuns' old address and check it out," she said. "The father could still live there. He might have an unlisted number now, and—"

"We have an unlisted number," Brian said, "because my mom is a cop."

Roni continued speaking as if she hadn't heard him. "—and if I can find the dad, maybe I can find out if Bryce Doblemun has any identifying marks, like a mole or something. Or like that scar on your elbow."

Brian covered the scar with his hand.

"You want to come?" Roni asked.

"Isn't Minneapolis out of bounds for you?"

"My mom didn't actually say how far I could go—she just made me promise not to go on major highways, but if I take the back roads, I'm technically not breaking the rules."

"Back roads? All the way to Minneapolis?"

"I mapped it out online. You in?"

Brian shook his head. "Can't."

"Why not?"

"Korean class. My parents won't tell me how they got me, but they want me to understand the cultural significance of who I really am."

11

cross-eyed baby

Roni congratulated herself on all the safety measures she had taken for this trip, the longest she had ever done on Hillary: helmet strapped on tight, full tank of gas, extra money, and a cell phone in case of utter emergency. Nick would be proud. Of course, she would kill her for making the trip in the first place—but even Nick would have to admit that Roni was well prepared.

The back-road route to Minneapolis was complicated, with lots of turns and stop signs. More than once, Roni thought she'd gotten lost, but soon the farm fields and horse pastures were replaced by SuperAmericas and Taco Bells, and she knew she was getting closer to the city. There was a lot of traffic—even the side streets had more traffic than downtown Bloodwater. Roni had only had one really close call when a big black Hummer pulled out in front of her. She had to slam on the brakes and cut onto the shoulder to avoid an accident. When Roni beeped her horn, the Hummer driver, talking on his cell phone, didn't even notice her.

It took almost two hours to reach the city, and another half hour to find Dight Avenue, a small street in the south-eastern part of the city. Roni drove slowly up Dight Avenue, counting down the house numbers on the east side of the street: 4523, 4521, 4519 . . . 4515, 4513 . . . Something was wrong.

She pulled over to the curb. Where was 4517? She parked her bike and walked back up the street to where 4517 Dight Avenue should have been.

It was a vacant lot.

Across the street, a middle-aged black man was washing his car at the curb. Roni walked over and said, "Nice car."

The man gave her the once-over. "Let me guess," he said. "You must be one of those Hells Angels."

Roni thought about what he was seeing: a slightly frumpy sixteen-year-old girl with a Vespa and a yellow motorcycle helmet. She grinned, and the man laughed.

"Nineteen seventy-four Lincoln Continental," he said, patting the hood of his car as if it were a prized pet. "They don't make 'em like this anymore."

"I can see you take really good care of it," Roni said.

"That's how come I still got it. Now, is there something I can help you with? You lost?"

"I'm looking for a man who used to live where that vacant lot is." She pointed at the vacant lot. "Did you know the family that lived there?"

He shook his head. "Sorry, can't help you. That house got tore down long ago, before I moved here. You might ask Irma Kelly, though. She's been here longer than anybody." He pointed out a small blue single-story house two lots down.

"Thanks." Roni walked down to Irma Kelly's and rang the doorbell. She saw a curtain move and caught a glimpse of white hair. The curtain closed. Roni rang the doorbell again, but nobody answered.

Discouraged, she walked back to the street. Just as she was trying to get up the courage to knock on another door, an SUV pulled up in front of the house next door. A thirty-something woman got out, opened the back door, unstrapped a baby from a car seat, and hoisted it up on her hip.

Roni walked over and introduced herself. "I'm trying to reach the man who used to live across the street from you. Lawrence Doblemun?"

"The Doblemuns. What a terrible story." The woman's brow crumpled. "It was before we moved here. Mrs. Doblemun ran off with their only child. Then the house burned down."

"Do you know what happened to Mr. Doblemun?"

"No. But I know who *would* know." She looked toward the house Roni had just been at. "Mrs. Kelly."

"I tried knocking on her door," Roni said. "She wouldn't answer."

The woman laughed. "Irma is a bit suspicious of strangers. Come on. I'll introduce you." Roni followed her up to Irma Kelly's door. The woman handed her baby to Roni and pressed the doorbell.

Roni didn't have a moment to say, "I don't know how to hold a baby, and I'm sure I might drop it." She looked at the drooling, cross-eyed baby. The baby stared back at her without blinking. Roni couldn't remember if she had ever held a baby before.

Looking down at it, she couldn't tell whether the creature was a boy or a girl. It stared at her with big brown eyes, then grabbed for her hair and yanked. The yank brought instant tears to Roni's eyes. The baby laughed. After untangling the little tyke's hand from her locks, Roni laughed, too.

The door opened. Irma Kelly peered out at them, a frail-looking woman with a cloud of thin white hair and greasy, oversize eyeglasses.

"Irma, this young lady has a question about the man who lived in the house that burned down."

"Lawrence Doblemun," Roni said.

"Lawrence, you say?" said the old woman. "The man lived in *that* house called his self *Lance.*"

"Do you know where he might have moved to?"

Irma Kelly squinted at Roni and said, "Now, why would a nice girl like you want to track down a man like Lance Doblemun?"

Roni thought fast. "I'm, um, I'm writing an article about child abductions in Minnesota," she said. "I'm interviewing parents who have lost their kids."

"Let me give you some advice, young lady." Irma Kelly crossed her thin arms and looked hard at Roni. Her eyes looked blurry and huge behind the lenses of her eyeglasses. "You give that man a wide berth. He was never no good, and I got no reason to think he's changed. You ask me, Vera Doblemun is well quit of him. I hope he never finds her."

"Do you know where he moved to after his house burned?"

Irma Kelly glared at Roni. "Did you hear a thing I said?"

"Yes, but I really need to find him for my article."

The old woman shook her head, then sighed and said, "Okay, I'll tell you where he lives—he did leave me a forwarding address—but promise me one thing."

"Anything," Roni said.

Irma Kelly shook her index finger at Roni. "Do not go to see him alone."

12
kimchi chick

The Korean teacher was a tall, thin man named Gee Jang. Short black hair stuck up from his head. He wore black-rimmed glasses, a black shirt, black jeans, white socks, and big shiny black shoes. Brian thought he looked like an exclamation point.

"I am glad for us to be here together today," Gee Jang said in a thick accent. "We will be going over practice of daily situational conversations. At the end of every class will be a session for help."

Brian was glad there would be a session for help; he knew he would need it. He wondered if the short time he had spent in Korea after his birth would give him any extra advantage. Maybe he had absorbed some of the culture from his crib.

The class contained twelve students. Ten looked like they might be Korean, and two were definitely not Korean. Most of the students were older than Brian, but there was one blond girl sitting to his left who looked about thirteen. When he had come into the classroom, she had smiled at him. Very friendly. She had big blue eyes and curly blond hair, which was cut short and looked like a halo around her head. She wasn't exactly pretty, but she was interesting looking—like someone who would have great stories to tell.

"Annyeong haseyo," she said, which meant "hello."

He said, *"Annyeong"* back to her, which was like saying "hi."

She was wearing a name tag that read MOLLY, and below that were some Korean letters. Brian guessed that was her name in Korean symbols. Brian didn't have a name tag yet. The Korean name he had chosen last year at language camp was Bok-Soo. That made him wonder how many names he'd had so far in his life: the name his birth mother gave him, the name his first adoptive mother gave him, his chosen Korean name, Bok-Soo, and now Brian, which could be the same name as his first American name, unless his name had been Bryce. Brian, Bryce—Roni was right. They were awfully close.

The time went fast as they learned how to say, "Please pass the kimchi" and "More tea for you?" There was an older woman in the class about his mom's age. She looked Korean. Brian found himself watching her, listening to her, wondering if she was anything like his Korean mother had been.

Before, he had rarely thought of his birth mother. Now he was thinking about that part of his life obsessively. It was all Roni's fault.

As the class broke up, Molly and an older Korean girl stood up and started walking out together. Just when she got to the door, Molly looked back and waved at him.

He waved back.

"Nice to see you again," she said, and she left the room.

Brian stood still. *Again?* What was that about? Had she been at the Korean language camp last summer? No way—he would have remembered her.

She must have him confused with somebody else.

Halfway back to Bloodwater, Roni got sick of following the little twisty back roads and turned onto Highway 61, the main highway from the Twin Cities to Bloodwater. The four-lane highway was scary, with cars and trucks whizzing past her, but it was a lot faster. She had only about fifteen miles to go when she noticed a sluggish feeling in Hillary's handlebars. Half a mile later a vibration set in, followed by a flapping sound. She pulled over to the shoulder and gazed bleakly at the front tire as it released its last gasp of air.

"This is not good," she said. Soybean fields stretched out on either side of the road. She took out her cell phone and checked for a signal. Three bars. That was good. But who to call? She didn't think Darwin Dipstick would be inclined to drive out to save her. She would have to call a garage in Hastings, which was only a few miles away, and hope that they could patch the tire again.

She was about to call directory assistance when a car pulled over to the shoulder. The passenger door opened and Brian Bain stepped out.

"Tire troubles, Holmes?"

Roni could have hugged him, but she resisted.

"Nothing a patch and a little air can't fix, Watson. What are you doing here?"

"We're driving home from my Korean class. I thought you were supposed to stay off the main highway."

"I was," Roni said.

Brian's dad got out of the car. "Roni. I see you are in a pneumatic quandary." He opened his trunk and pulled out a large aerosol can. "Would a shot of Flat-B-Gone help?"

Roni drove most of the way back to Bloodwater on the shoulder, keeping her speed below twenty-five. Brian and his dad followed. Mr. Bain was concerned that Roni's tire would go flat again. The Flat-B-Gone had reinflated and sealed the tire, but it was a temporary fix, at best.

Brian wanted to ride with Roni, but Roni hadn't brought an extra helmet, so that was out. It was driving him crazy not to be able to talk to her about her trip to Minneapolis. When they got to Darwin Dipstick's garage, Brian jumped out of the car and told his dad he'd walk home from there.

"So what's the story?" he asked Roni.

Roni pulled off her helmet and shook out her hair. "I thought you didn't care about the Doblemuns," she said.

"I don't. But I'm curious. Did you find the house?"

"Let me talk to Darwin first, then I'll tell you what I found."

Roni's new tire had arrived that afternoon. Darwin promised to install it first thing in the morning. As Brian walked Roni home, she told him what she had learned.

"The address turned out to be a vacant lot. The house burned down nine years ago."

"Oh."

"But I found out where Mr. Lance Doblemun lives. Guess."

"Tierra del Fuego?"

"According to Mrs. Irma Kelly, he lives in Pepin," Roni said.

"Pepin, Wisconsin?" Pepin was only about thirty miles away, just on the other side of the river.

"Exactly. I'm going there to find him, first thing in the morning—as soon as Darwin puts on my new tire. And you have to come with me."

"I do? Why?"

"I promised Irma Kelly that I wouldn't go alone."

13

go back lane

"How come you never let me drive?" Brian shouted in Roni's ear.

"Because you're not old enough, because you don't have a license, and because I'm a better driver," Roni said over her shoulder.

"How do you know?"

"I just do." Roni had shown Brian how to ride Hillary a few weeks earlier, letting him tool around in an empty church parking lot. Now she was wishing she hadn't. The kid wouldn't leave her alone.

"I think I'm very talented," Brian said. "Like Evel Knievel."

"That does *not* make me want you in the driver's seat. Anyway, we're already here." She pointed at the green sign welcoming them to Pepin, Wisconsin. According to the sign, 883 people lived there. Roni cruised slowly down the main thoroughfare. Pepin was a typical river town, with the highway serving as the main street, a mix of businesses and houses on each side, and a bunch of side streets poking out from it like legs on a centipede.

"What now?" Brian asked.

"Now we ask somebody," Roni said as she pulled into a convenience store/gas station and parked. "There are only a few hundred people here. If we ask enough of them, we're bound to find somebody who knows Lance Doblemun."

They climbed off of Hillary.

"Nice butt massage," said Brian, rubbing his hind end with both hands. Roni's rear was a little numb, too. Forty minutes on a Vespa was a whole lot of shaking.

"I'll just run in and ask the clerk if he knows any Doblemuns," Roni said. "You stay here and guard Hillary."

"Guard her from what?"

"Thieves, vandals . . . porcupines."

"Why porcupines?"

"I don't need another flat tire. Watch out for sharp, pokey objects of all kinds."

Inside the store, three men wearing Green Bay Packers caps were gathered at the counter chatting with the clerk. Roni waited for them to finish their business so she could talk to the clerk, a hefty woman with three chins and a cap of frizzy blond hair. After about two minutes it became apparent that the men were not there to buy anything—they were just talking.

"Excuse me," Roni said.

They all turned to look at her.

"I'm trying to find someone, and I was hoping you could help me," she said to the clerk.

"Who are you looking for, dear?"

"A man named Lawrence Doblemun. He might use the name Lance Doblemun."

"Doblemun. Hmm." She stroked her chins. "He lives here in Pepin?"

"I think so."

"Bert, you know any Doblemuns hereabouts?"

One of the men tipped his hat back and scratched under the bill. "I know a Dobbins, and a Davidson, and a Duggan. Any of them do ya?"

Roni shook her head.

One of the other men said, "We got a fella named Monk. If there was two of him, you'd have Double Monk."

The third man said, "I used to know a guy named Lance, only his last name was Boyle. Lance Boyle."

Realizing that they were playing with her, Roni felt her face grow red. "Thanks anyway." She turned and went back outside, trying not to let their chuckles bother her.

Brian was not guarding Hillary. Great. She looked around and found him at the other end of the building, standing at a pay phone. He was writing something on his hand.

"Hey!" she yelled. "I'm about to steal this here motorcycle!"

Brian looked up, then trotted over to her. "Any luck?" he asked.

"No. We'll have to ask someplace else. . . . What are you grinning about?"

Brian shoved his hand in her face. Something was written on his palm in blue ink.

"Ten twenty-six Goatback Lane," Roni read. "What's that?"

"Lawrence Doblemun's address. It was in the Pepin phone book."

Brian loved to one-up Roni. She would get all scowly and sarcastic for a few minutes, and then she would say something like "I was about to check the phone book myself," which he knew was probably not true.

"I wonder where Goatback Lane is," he said.

"I suppose I could go back inside and ask," Roni said, but she showed no inclination to do so. Brian got the feeling that the people inside the store had not been friendly.

He said, "Since the address is written on my hand, I'll ask." He headed into the store, where he found three old guys and a lady clerk scratching off lottery tickets.

"Any luck?" Brian said.

"Not hardly," said one of the men, ripping his ticket in half.

Brian held out his hand, showing the address he had written there.

"What's that you got there, son? A tattoo?"

"An address I'm looking for. Anybody know where Goatback Lane is?"

"Just down the street from Hogbelly Hollow," said one of the men. Everybody laughed, including Brian.

"What's on Goatback Lane?" asked the woman behind the counter.

“I’m visiting a friend,” Brian said.

“I didn’t think *anybody* lived on Goatback,” said the man who had ripped up the lottery ticket. “Nothing up there but coulees, bluffs, and rattlesnakes.”

“It’s not here in Pepin?” Brian asked.

“Pepin *County*, maybe,” he said.

Brian took out his blue felt-tip pen and poised it over his forearm. “How do I get there?”

“Are you sure you wrote it down right?” Roni yelled over her shoulder.

“Yes,” Brian yelled back. “But I can’t guarantee they gave me the right directions. We should have seen the sign for Goatback Lane by now.”

They had taken a road called CC to a road called XX to yet another road called, simply, Z. For some reason, Wisconsin named its county roads with letters instead of names or numbers.

“They said there was a sign,” Brian said.

“I haven’t seen anything but deer trails and poison ivy,” Roni said.

“Slow down—what’s that?”

Roni throttled back as they came to a road leading off to the left. She came to a complete stop. The road was marked by a barely legible sign on a rusted metal post:

GOATBACK LANE

"What do you think?" Roni asked.

"I get the feeling that Lance Doblemun is not a people person."

"One way to find out." Roni revved the engine and they turned onto Goatback Lane, a steep, twisted dirt road that climbed slowly but relentlessly toward the top of the bluffs.

14

squirrel skulls

About a mile later, Roni and Brian came to a driveway marked by a sagging mailbox with several small skulls nailed to its post. L. DOBLEMUN was painted on the side of the box. Brian hopped off the bike for a closer look.

"Squirrel skulls," he said.

"He must not like rodents," Roni said.

The driveway was little more than a pair of tire tracks weaving through the woods, so narrow that if a car came from the opposite direction they would be forced into the tangled brush lining the trail. At one point they were stopped by a tree trunk about six inches in diameter that had fallen across the trail. They had to get off the Vespa and lift it over one wheel at a time to proceed.

"Tell me again what we're doing here," Brian said.

"We're here to see if Lance Doblemun was your first adoptive father," Roni said. "Maybe you'll recognize him."

"The guy I remember was jolly. I don't think he'd nail squirrel skulls to his mailbox."

The driveway ended in a clearing about two hundred feet across. Roni stopped her Vespa at the edge of the woods. At the far side of the clearing was a dilapidated mobile home, once a cheerful shade of yellow, the paint now peeling from the bare aluminum like skin from a bad sunburn. An equally dilapidated pickup truck was parked in front, next to a smoking metal barbecue.

"Just in time for lunch, I guess," said Roni, turning off the engine.

The mobile home door banged open and a tall, thin, bearded man came out carrying what looked like a slab of meat.

"What's he got?" Roni whispered.

"Looks like a dead squirrel," Brian said.

The man lifted the lid of the barbecue and laid the dead squirrel—or whatever it was—on the hot grill, then went back inside, wiping his hands on his faded coveralls.

"Does he look familiar?" Roni asked.

"I can't tell," Brian said. "He's got that beard covering half his face."

"I suppose we could ask him to shave it off."

"Right."

Roni put down the kickstand and hopped off the Vespa. "You stay here. I'll go talk to him."

"What are you going to say?"

"I'll improvise." She marched across the field to the mobile home. She could hear the man humming to himself inside—some sort of geriatric rock 'n' roll, seriously off-key. Dozens of empty beer cans littered the trampled grass around the mobile home. Roni rapped on the door.

The humming instantly stopped. Roni stepped back a few paces, waiting.

The door banged open. The bearded man stood there holding a cast-iron frying pan in one hand.

"Who are YOU?" he said in a voice like a shovel full of gravel.

Roni had interviewed irascible older men before. She knew better than to show fear. But in fact, she was terrified. Up close, Lance Doblemun looked in even rougher shape than his paint-deprived home. His eyes were red, his teeth were stained brown, his left eye pointed in the wrong direction, his clothing was filthy, and his odor—it took a second for it to hit her—was like bad cheese on week-old fish.

Clearly, he was not prepared to receive guests.

"I'm Roni Delicata," Roni said. "Are you Mr. Lawrence Doblemun?"

"What if I am? And it's *Lance,* not *Lawrence.*"

A second wave of stink hit Roni's nostrils, one she recognized immediately: alcohol. Lance Doblemun was thoroughly pickled.

Roni took a few steps back, keeping about six feet between them. She thought she could outrun him, but she wasn't sure.

"If you're the county assessor, you can just stick your fascist tax bill where the sun don't shine, missy. I told them, next government man sets foot on my land I'm gonna put the Oshkosh b'gosh on 'em."

"I'm not a tax collector, Mr. Doblemun."

"That's what the last one said." He advanced a few more drunken steps. "Set my dog on him, that one."

Dog? Roni looked around frantically. There was no way she could outrun a dog.

She said, "Mr. Doblemun, if you ever want to see your son Bryce again, you'd better behave yourself."

15

pop

“What do you know about Bry?” Lance Doblemun said, squinting at Roni.

“So you never found him?”

“If I knew where he was, you think I’d be living in this dump?” He shook his head as if he wanted the thought to go away. “He’s been gone ten years. I gave up on him.”

“If you gave up, then why do you have his picture posted on the missing-children website?”

Doblemun snorted. “First I heard about that! Probably my busybody witch of a mother-in-law.” He tipped his head, focusing on her with his good eye. “Why? Do you know something?”

“I’m an investigator,” Roni said, taking out her notebook. “I’m looking into several missing-children cases, and I wanted to check on a few things. How long did he live with you?”

“About three years.”

“Did he have any identifying marks? Scars? Birthmarks?”

"Nah, the kid was perfect."

"I understand that Bryce might have been taken by your wife."

"That's what always happens, the police say. Me and the wife were having problems, you know, not getting along so good. The kid was her idea. She thought getting a Chinese kid would help our relationship. Fat chance."

"I thought Bryce was Korean," Roni said.

"Korean, Chinese, same difference."

Roni made a note. Maybe Irma Kelly was right—Mrs. Doblemun may have had good reason to run off with her child.

Doblemun was getting impatient. "So what do you got to tell me? You know something about Bry?"

"Just a few more questions," Roni said.

"I don't think so," Doblemun said. He moved faster than Roni had thought possible—one quick stride, and his free hand shot out and clamped around her wrist. He pulled her up against him.

"My turn to ask the questions, missy."

It was driving Brian crazy not being able to hear a word they were saying. He was considering sneaking around through the woods when suddenly Lance Doblemun grabbed Roni and started dragging her toward the mobile home.

Brian didn't hesitate: He jumped on the Vespa and started it. In seconds he was flying across the clearing, straight at

Roni and her captor. He waited until the last possible second, then hit the brake and skidded to a stop. Roni and the bearded man both stared at him.

Brian didn't want to get any closer, but he had to give Roni a chance to get away. He decided to try something.

"Hey, Pop," he yelled.

The man released his grip on Roni's arm, and she backed quickly away from him.

"Bry . . . ?" said the man.

It sent a shiver up Brian's spine to hear this derelict of a human being call him *Bry,* which could easily be his own nickname.

Doblemun took a step toward him; Brian twisted the accelerator, the rear wheel spun, and an instant later he was speeding back across the clearing. Lance Doblemun ran after him. Brian kept the bike going just fast enough to stay out of his reach. When he was almost to the trail leading out of the clearing, he made a wide loop and headed back toward the mobile home.

Roni saw what Brian was doing. She ran an intercept course and hopped on the back of the Vespa when he got to her. Doblemun was also trying to run an interception, but Brian spun the bike around and took off at a right angle, again aiming for the exit road. Doblemun tried to change direction, but lost his footing and fell headlong in the grass.

Brian stopped the bike and looked back across the clearing. The man was climbing to his feet, but there was no way he could catch them now.

"Hey!" Brian yelled. "Your squirrel is burning!"

The man shook his fist, then ran back toward the mobile home.

Brian laughed.

Roni said, "Get going! Hurry! He's got a dog!"

Brian took off down Goatback Lane. Behind them, they heard the howl of what sounded like an enormous hound.

"Faster!" Roni yelled.

Brian twisted the accelerator.

"Slow down!" Roni yelled.

"Make up your mind!" Brian said—then he saw what Roni had just remembered: the fallen log crossing the trail. He just had time to say "uh—" when the world turned upside down.

16

upended

Hillary's front tire hit the log hard. The Vespa stopped, but Roni and Brian kept going. Roni landed in a prickly bush a few yards away. Flailing at the branches, she quickly managed to extract herself.

"Brian?" she called out.

"Over here." Brian was clawing his way out of a hazelnut bush. "Are you all right?"

"I think so."

A loud howl caused them both to scramble to their feet. The giant hound was getting closer. Roni ran to the Vespa and lifted it upright. Amazingly, the engine was still running.

"Is it okay?" Brian asked.

"I think so. Get on!"

Just as Brian was throwing his leg over the seat, the dog appeared around the bend of the driveway and let out an excited bellow.

Brian started to laugh. The big noise was coming from a small, floppy-eared basset hound. The dog skidded to a stop a few yards away from them and commenced a series of barks, howls, bellows, and snorts.

"Good dog!" said Brian.

The hound wagged his short tail.

"He won't hurt us," Brian said.

"Yeah, but—" They heard the roar of a truck engine coming down the driveway.

"Go! Go!" Brian yelled, wrapping his arms around Roni's waist.

Roni twisted the accelerator and they took off down the driveway. The hound howled and was joined by a disturbing squeal from Hillary's front wheel.

Brian looked back as Lance Doblemun's battered pickup truck appeared about a hundred feet back, gaining on them. The hound jumped out of the way of the truck with an indignant yelp.

"Faster!" Brian shouted in Roni's ear.

"Shut *up*!" she yelled back.

Brian didn't think they could count on Lance Doblemun stopping when he caught up, but he had only a second to worry about it before the truck hit the log. The front end bounced into the air and came down with a loud metallic crunch. The truck skidded to a stop, its front end askew. The last thing Brian saw as they rounded a bend in the driveway was Lance Doblemun's face, contorted with anger and frustration.

Roni refused to stop until they were back on Highway 35, heading out of Pepin. Once she was sure they weren't being followed, she pulled into a wayside rest and parked.

"Where's your helmet?" Roni asked.

Brian's hand flew to the top of his head. "I think I lost it at Doblemun's place." He grinned. "Want to go back and get it?"

"No way." Roni shuddered.

They sat on the low stone wall that circled the parking lot. A hundred feet below them, on the other side of the railroad tracks, was Lake Pepin, a twenty-mile-long wide spot in the Mississippi. Several small boats—some with sails, others powered by engines—traveled up and down the busy waterway. Some of them might be heading for the Gulf of Mexico. It all looked so peaceful—Roni found it hard to believe that only minutes before they had nearly been run over by a drunk in a pickup truck.

She said, "That was brilliant when you called him Pop."

"I just wanted him to let go of you."

"So do you think he was?"

"Was what?"

"Your pop."

"Not in a million years. There wasn't a single molecule of pop-ness in him."

"Not even one molecule?"

"I never saw the guy before in my life."

17

darwin, again

Hillary's front wheel had not mended itself during their short rest stop. Every time Roni tried to speed up past twenty miles per hour, the noise would go from a mildly distressing *squee-squee-squee* to an outright alarming *skreeeeeeeonk*!

Brian, at his irritating best, shouted his theories into her right ear.

"I bet it's a bent axle!"

"Shut *up*!"

"Or it could be the bearings. If the bearings get too hot, the wheel could fall off."

"Shut UP!"

"Maybe the tire is rubbing on something. You should—"

That was when Roni snapped her helmeted head back and bonked him on the nose. Brian let out a yelp. She was immediately sorry she'd done it, and said so.

"After I save your life and everything, you bonk me," Brian said.

"Just don't talk about my wheel falling off while we're rolling," Roni said. "It's bad luck."

"I think you broke my nose."

"You've survived two encounters with homicidal bushes this week—what's a little helmet bonk?"

"I should bonk *you.*"

"Not while I'm driving."

"Fine. I owe you one bonk."

When they finally limped into Bloodwater, Roni drove straight to Darwin's garage. He was not happy to see them again.

"You kids got to learn to treat your machines better," he said, shaking his head as he examined the front wheel. "Just 'cause you got a brand-new tire up front don't mean you can go banging into stuff. It's disrespectful. Now you've gone and bent the axle."

"Told you," said Brian.

"You told me it was about six *different* things," Roni said.

"Lucky you didn't kill yourselves doing whatever it was you done," Darwin said.

"Can you fix it?" Roni asked.

"I can fix anything. Don't know when I'll have time, though. Got a letter from the mayor's office yesterday telling me to clean up my backyard."

"You mean your *junk*yard," Roni said.

"Apparently, some citizen called and complained."

"It wasn't me," Roni said.

"You know how long it took me last time to straighten up

my valuable auto parts inventory? Not to mention cutting those weeds back. I'll be back there for days!"

"So when can you fix my bike?"

Darwin frowned, shaking his head. "You might want to find yourself alternative transport for the next couple-few weeks."

18

the foundling

Brian was tired of all the guessing games. He planned to question his parents at dinner. He wouldn't stop until he got the whole truth out of them, once and for all.

But like many of his best-laid schemes, nothing went quite the way he planned.

First his mom called and said she would be late.

"How late?" he asked.

"Oh, I don't know. You two go ahead and eat without me."

"We'll wait for you," he said. If she knew they were waiting, she might get home sooner. "We're making a surprise dinner."

"Oh . . . how nice!"

The strain in his mother's voice reminded Brian of the last surprise dinner he and his dad had prepared.

"No Catfish Banana Surprise this time," he promised.

"Thank you. And please, no flammable desserts," his mother added before hanging up.

Now all he had to do was come up with an edible, fire-safe surprise that contained neither catfish nor bananas.

Brian flipped through some of his mom's cookbooks until he found a picture of something that looked tasty. He brought the book to his dad, who was in his office peering at the windowsill through a powerful magnifying glass.

"What are you looking at?" Brian asked.

Mr. Bain jumped, almost dropping the magnifying glass. "Oh, hello, son," he said with a sheepish smile. "I was looking at the dust gathered on the sill. Fascinating stuff, dust."

Brian plunked the open cookbook down on the dusty sill. "For dinner," he said. "I told Mom we were making her a surprise."

Mr. Bain frowned. "You know how your mother feels about surprises."

"She likes them if they taste good."

"Yes, but . . . chocolate soufflé? For dinner?"

"Why not?"

"Isn't timing rather critical in making a soufflé? We never know when your mother will arrive home."

"True. Maybe we should create a new hotdish." Every once in a while he and his dad would try a new combination of food products to make a new hotdish. The clam-and-spinach hotdish had turned out okay, but the pumpkin-pecan hotdish had been nearly as inedible as the Catfish Banana Surprise.

Mr. Bain checked out the cupboards while Brian looked in the refrigerator. One of the rules of their collaborations was that they couldn't go to the store. They had to use what was on hand.

Brian came out with jar of olives and some pepperoni; his dad held up some rigatoni and a can of tomatoes.

His father boiled the rigatoni noodles while Brian sliced the olives and pepperoni. Then they mixed it all together with the canned tomatoes, added a little garlic and oregano, topped it with a cup of cheese, and put it in the oven on low.

Two hours later, Mrs. Bain showed up. She looked closely at Brian's face and said, "Do I detect some fresh scratches on my precious child?"

"The bushes are out to get me," Brian said. He did not mention that the latest bush had been in Pepin, Wisconsin.

"Hmm," his mother said with a frown.

They hauled the hotdish out of the oven. Brian served up a big mound of it on each of their plates. It looked okay.

They all took a bite.

"Mmm," his mother said while chewing.

"Not bad. Maybe another gram or two of salt," his father said.

"It tastes like pizza," Brian said. "Pizza hotdish."

"I think this one goes in the repertoire," his mom said.

In that short lull after they had all finished eating, but before they jumped up to clear the table, Brian asked his question. "Okay, so when and how did you adopt me?"

"Brian . . . ," his mother started.

"I'm serious," Brian said. "What's the big secret? I mean, it's my life."

"He's right, dear," said Mr. Bain.

Mrs. Bain sighed and seemed to sink into her chair.

Mr. Bain said, "Brian, as you have already deduced, we were not the first couple to adopt you. You came to America and were adopted by a couple named Owen and Janice Samuels. The Samuelses were part of a group of Minnesotans who arranged to adopt homeless children from Korea. You were about five months old when they brought you here."

"Here? You mean like here in Bloodwater?"

"No, the Samuelses lived in Cannon Falls, twenty miles away."

"What happened to them? Why did they give me up?" Brian felt his eyes getting wet. He didn't care.

"Son, there was an accident. A car accident. Both Owen and Janice were killed. You were at home with a babysitter the night of the accident. You were only three."

Nobody spoke for several long seconds.

"What about Sniffer? Did I really have a dog?"

Now his mom started crying. Brian looked at his dad. If his dad started crying, too, he was afraid the world would end. But Mr. Bain maintained his usual slightly distracted, slightly puzzled demeanor.

"You did have a dog, son. He went to live with another family."

"So how did I end up with you?"

"We knew the Samuelses," said Brian's mother, suppressing a sob. "Janice was a school friend of mine. We knew you, too. You were such a sweet child. Janice and Owen were so happy when you came into their lives. They told us that if anything ever happened to them, they hoped we would adopt you. So when . . . when they died, we did."

"Because you told them you would?"

"Because we wanted to."

"Why didn't you ever tell me?"

"You were so unhappy, son," his father said. "You missed the Samuelses terribly, and you didn't understand why you couldn't see them."

"You looked for that little dog every day for weeks on end," his mother added. "Wandering through the house calling, '*Sniffer? Sniiiiffer?*' Over and over again. It about broke my heart."

"Eventually you seemed to forget about them, and we just didn't want to remind you. We decided to wait until you were older . . . and now I guess you are."

Brian wiped his sleeve across his eyes. He hadn't even realized he had been crying.

Mrs. Bain said, "I'm sorry we kept this from you, Brian. You deserve to know about your past. It was just so easy to put off telling you. We didn't want to hurt you."

"Is there anything else you haven't told me?" Brian asked.

His mother sat back in her chair. "What else do you want to know?"

"How come my Korean mom gave me away?"

"We don't really know, Brian. You were a foundling. You were left on the steps of a police station in Taegu City, South Korea."

"I was *dumped*?"

"Most likely your mother was very poor, son," his dad said. "She probably left you because she hoped you would be adopted by a family that could give you a chance for a better life."

"She must not have been a very good person," Brian said. "What kind of mother would dump her own kid at the police station?"

"Not a bad place to leave a kid," said his mother, who was very proud of her chosen profession.

"Yeah, but . . . so even if I wanted to, I could never find out who my real mother is?"

"I'm afraid not," his dad said.

Brian nodded, trying to accept the cold, hard facts, when something hit him like a fist to the gut.

"So we don't even know for sure what day I was born!" he said. "I don't even have a real birthday?"

"Of course you do," his mother said.

"We just don't know exactly when it is," his father added.

19

the art of the whine

Roni usually got along pretty well with her mother. Except when Nick was being unreasonable.

"Mom, it's only three dollars each to download articles from the *Star Tribune,* and I only need to order a few—but I have to give them a credit card number. I'll pay you back."

"I don't know, Roni. I'm just not comfortable letting you use my credit card online. Besides, you already owe me forty dollars for that motorcycle tire."

"It's not a motorcycle. It's a motor *scooter*. And this isn't for Hillary, it's for *research*."

"Nevertheless—"

"How will I learn fiscal responsibility if you don't give me a chance?"

Roni whined all during breakfast. She whined as she washed the dishes. She whined as she watched her mother pack her briefcase to drive downtown to the mayor's office. She was following her mother out to her car, still whining, when Nick Delicata made a sputtering sound with her lips, pulled her wallet out of her purse, and held out her Visa card.

"Not one penny more than twenty dollars goes on this card or I'll have your hide."

"Thank you thank you thank you thank you thank you thank you thank you!" Roni said. "You're the best mom in the world."

"You have to promise me one more thing."

"Anything!"

"I want two solid weeks without once having to listen to you whine. About *anything.* I don't know how you can stand to listen to yourself sometimes."

Roni snatched the card. "Deal." She ran back into the house, thinking that there was a very good reason why kids whine.

Because it works.

Brian remembered his dreams. He had dreamed about the big laughing man, and the smiling woman with the red hair, and the little dog—but now he knew they weren't just dreams. The Samuelses were real. It made him feel more real, too.

He waited until after noon to call Roni—she could be cranky in the morning. When she answered the phone, he said, "Guess who I am."

"Tiger Woods."

"Why Tiger Woods?"

"I think he's cute."

"Actually, I'm Brian Samuels. At least that's who I used to be."

Roni didn't say anything for several heartbeats. "That sounds portentous."

"What's *portentous*?"

"It means, like, ominous and full of meaning."

"Meet at the marina? End of the pier?" Brian said.

"Give me half an hour," Roni said. "I'm reduced to travel by foot."

"Ah, yes. Poor Hillary."

"Poor Roni, you mean."

Roni preferred it when she was the one to deliver earth-shattering news to Brian, not the other way around, so before leaving, she printed out three of the articles she had found in the *Star Tribune* archives. First was an article about the abduction, showing a photo of the three-and-a-half-year-old Bryce Doblemun. The second article, dated a few weeks later, was a short human-interest piece about the Doblemuns' house burning down. Lawrence Doblemun was portrayed as a tragic figure who had lost his wife, his child, and now his home. The article included a photo of a younger, beardless Lawrence Doblemun standing in front of the burned-down house.

The third article, several months later, said that Lawrence Doblemun had been charged with burning down his own house to collect the insurance money.

20

pebbles

"So, you see, there's no mystery," Brian said after telling Roni what he had learned from his parents.

Roni stared at him. "No mystery? Are you crazy?"

"Nope. Perfectly sane." They were sitting on the end-most dock at Bloodwater Marina, looking out across the Mississippi. Brian threw a pebble into the water. A gull sailed low over the widening ripples. Sometimes people threw pieces of bread, or fish guts, or some other delicacy. This time, the gull was disappointed.

"You don't even know who you are!" Roni said.

"I am Brian Bain, formerly Brian Samuels."

"Yeah, and you were found on the steps of a Korean police station. Who were you then? And why did your parents *lie* to you?"

"I guess I was pretty messed up after the Samuelses died. They just thought it would be better for me to forget. It's not like there's some huge conspiracy." He tossed out another pebble. The gull returned, once again hoping for a scrap of food. "It's kinda sad. I mean, I *knew* them, but I didn't *know* them, if you know what I mean." He threw another pebble. This time, the gull ignored the splash.

"Give me a pebble," Roni said.

"Why?"

"So I can have fun teasing the seagull, too."

"I told you to pick some up as we were crossing the parking lot, but no, you couldn't be bothered, and now you can just sit there and watch as I toss my pebbles and watch the ripples move out from them in perfect concentric circles."

Roni held out her hand. Brian made her wait a couple of seconds, then slowly counted out two pebbles and placed them in her hand as if they were gold coins.

Roni tossed out both pebbles at once, but even the double splash did not entice the gull to return. The ripples faded into the river.

"So I guess that's that," Brian said.

"What's what?"

"The great doppelganger mystery is over."

"Not by half. We still don't know what happened to Bryce Doblemun—"

"Vera Doblemun abducted him to get him away from her creepy husband. Besides, the police have had the case for ten years and gotten nowhere."

"—or why he looks so much like you. And what about the orange-haired lady?"

"What orange-haired lady?"

"Darwin said there was an orange-haired lady asking where you lived."

"There was?"

"I didn't tell you," Roni said.

"Why not?"

"I forgot. Oh, and I might have seen her. I mean, I saw this orange-haired lady at the library a couple of days ago."

"And she was asking about *me*?"

"I don't know. She was talking really loud, and Ms. Paige sort of ignored her, so she took off in a huff."

"Why would she be looking for me?"

"I don't know. Maybe it's something to do with the paper-airplane article."

"Weird." Brian tossed out his last pebble, stood up, and picked up his skateboard. "If I see her, I'll ask her what she wants. As far as Bryce Doblemun's concerned, we don't even know what he looks like now, or even if he's still alive. That age-progressed picture is just somebody's guess. In ten years he could have gotten fat or thin or have really bad acne or weird crooked teeth or who knows. But at least I know I'm not him." He started to walk away.

"Wait, I didn't show you what I found!" Roni jumped up and ran after him. She pulled the newspaper articles from her pocket and shoved them at him. "I found the article about the kidnapping. Here's a picture of Lance Doblemun."

Brian looked at the photo. "He looks better without the beard, but I still don't know him."

"Keep reading. The guy burned his own house down to collect the insurance."

"How come he's not in jail, then?"

"He got off on some technicality."

Brian skimmed the articles and handed the papers back to Roni. "So what? We already knew he was a creep. None of this has anything to do with me." He started walking away again.

Roni said, "Yeah, but—"

Brian spun around and faced her. "What's your problem? None of this matters! I don't want to know any more. Okay, so my parents were wrong not to tell me about my first parents, but now they have. Mystery solved."

"You're giving up? I spent my mom's hard-earned cash to get these stories about what happened to Bryce. Aren't you even interested?"

"What you don't seem to get, Miss Shirley Holmes, is that this is my *life,* not some stupid newspaper article you want to write." He walked away, skateboard under his arm.

"I'm not giving up," Roni said.

"Fine." Brian kept walking.

Roni followed Brian down the long dock to the parking lot, wishing she'd kept one of the pebbles—or a brick—to throw at him. She hoped Lance Doblemun would come running up and kidnap him and drag him off to some cave. Brian would want her on the case *then.* She watched him drop his skateboard when he reached the parking lot, put one foot on it, and push off. He thought he was so cool. He had no idea how dorky he looked.

What she was really mad about was that she had no idea how to go about finding Bryce Doblemun. He was just a missing kid who happened to look like Brian. Maybe Brian was right—maybe it was over. Brian had learned everything there was to learn about his past, and without her help. Now she was at a dead end. P. Q. Delicata, teenage reporter, had reverted to Roni Delicata, teenage schlump.

It made her furious.

Brian, rolling across the none-too-smooth parking lot, looked as if he would topple at any moment. So far he was staying on his board, holding his arms out for balance, acting as if he were going a million miles an hour down a huge hill when he was only going as fast as most people could walk.

Just then, Roni noticed she wasn't the only person watching Brian. A woman sitting in a little green car had her eyes fastened on him. Roni decided to try to get a little closer and see if she could get a good look at the woman.

She nonchalantly walked across the parking lot to get a better view. It definitely was not the old orange-haired woman. This woman had long black hair. She appeared to be Asian, maybe in her late twenties or early thirties. The woman watched Brian until he reached the street and turned onto the sidewalk. As soon as he disappeared from view, she pulled out of her parking space and started after him.

Roni yelled, "Hey!" She ran toward the car.

The woman looked at Roni, startled, then tromped on her accelerator and roared out of the parking lot, tires spinning, barely checking to see if any other cars were coming.

Heart pounding, Roni pulled out her trusty notebook and pencil and scrawled down the woman's license plate number.

21

ojinx-o teegim

The next day, Brian managed to avoid thinking about his adoption, about Lance Doblemun, or about Roni Delicata. He did this by designing two new paper airplanes, then spending a few hours at the skate park trying to learn the ollie kickflip, which looked easy but turned out to be—as near as Brian could tell—impossible. Instead of learning a cool new maneuver, he learned that repeated falls on a concrete surface could result in some truly spectacular bruises. He limped home defeated.

The next morning, he came downstairs with his skateboard ready to try again, but his mother intercepted him.

"Brian! Is that what you're wearing?"

"Uh . . . yeah?"

"You have to leave for Korean class in ten minutes!"

"I was just there!"

"That was three days ago. The class meets twice a week."

"But I—"

"Brian, this is not up for negotiation. Besides, your father has a surprise for you on the way home."

"What surprise?"

"If we told you, it wouldn't be a surprise."

Brian groaned and trudged upstairs to change his clothes.

Once again, Gee Jang was dressed like an exclamation point, right down to the white socks. Brian wondered if there was a way to tell him he looked like a punctuation mark without offending him. Probably not.

"Today," he said, "we talk about Korean family, and social customs of the street. At end of class we be a Korean lunch table."

Brian thought of asking him exactly what a Korean lunch table was and why he would want to be one, but he knew he needed to work on his attitude.

Gee Jang went on about Korean familial relationships, and which side of the street to walk on in Seoul, and how to order *bulgogi* or *bibimbop* in a Korean restaurant. All of which Brian found supremely uninteresting, since he never planned to go to Korea. Why should he? His mother had dumped him on the steps at a police station. There was no way he could ever find her, not even if he wanted to. Not even if he put Roni Delicata on the case.

Brian looked around at the other students to see if they were as bored as he was. Most of them were taking notes. The blond girl, Molly, listened intently to every word from Gee Jang's mouth. What was *her* deal?

They took a break after the first hour. One of the women

who worked at the center had laid out a spread of Korean snacks in the lunchroom. All the food was weird. He selected something called *ojinx-o teegim* because it looked almost normal—sort of like thick rectangular potato chips. Seeing Molly sitting alone at one of the tables, Brian walked over to her, trying unsuccessfully to remember how to say, "May I join you?" in Korean.

Resorting to English, he said, "Can I sit here?"

"Sure!" Molly smiled at him. She had a mischievous, troublemaking smile that appealed to him.

"What have you got there?" she asked.

"Ojinx-o teegim," said Brian, mangling the pronunciation.

"I got the *p'ajon,*" she said. "Onion pancake squares."

Brian made a face.

"They're good," she said.

"I guess, if you like onion." Brian watched her take a bite, then asked, "So what part of Korea are *you* from?"

Molly laughed. "I'm here for my brother," she said. "My family just adopted a two-year-old boy from Seoul. I decided to learn everything I could about Korea so when he gets older I can teach him about where he came from. How about you?"

"I got dumped on the steps of the police station in Taegu City."

"Really? I was a foundling, too! My parents adopted me from Romania."

"Cool," said Brian, although there wasn't anything cool

about being dumped. He picked up one of his chips and started to put it in his mouth.

"I didn't think I'd ever see you again," Molly said.

Brian lowered the chip and stared at her.

"I like you with the shorter hair," she said.

"Um . . . I think maybe you think I'm somebody else," he said.

She peered at him closely. "Really?"

"Seriously, where do you think you know me from?"

"The Korean Cultural Center? In St. Paul?"

Brian shook his head. "I've never been there."

"Wow," Molly said. "You look just like him. Except for the hair. And he had an earring."

Brian felt his heart starting to race.

"What was his name?"

"Dak-Ho. What's your name?"

"Brian."

"What's your Korean name?"

"Bok-Soo. What about this guy's American name? The one who looks like me."

"Billy."

"Billy," said Brian thoughtfully. He put the chip he had been holding into his mouth and bit down. Whatever it was, it was not a potato chip. It had the texture of a rubber band, and it tasted fishy. Brian didn't want to spit it out in front of Molly, so he forced himself to chew and swallow. It wasn't easy. Once he got it down, he looked at the other chips on his plate, then at Molly, who had an impish grin on her face.

"What did I just eat?" he asked.

"*Ojinx-o teegim* means 'fried squid finger food,'" Molly said. She laughed at Brian's expression, then pushed her plate toward him. "Have some onion pancake," she said. "It'll wash away the taste."

It took Roni two days to get Officer Garth Spall alone. Every time she saw him, he was with his partner, George Firth. George Firth, a veteran of the Bloodwater Police Department, knew Roni too well. If she asked him for a favor, he would, first, refuse to do it, and second, probably mention it to Nick. Garth Spall—younger, less experienced, and several dozen points lower in the IQ department—would be more cooperative.

She finally caught Garth alone in his squad car in the alley behind Bratten's Café and Bakery, working his way through a bag of donuts. He was a tall, athletic young man with overdeveloped muscles and a weakness for raised glazed donuts. Roni walked up to the passenger window and looked in at him. He was staring dreamily off into the distance while shoving a donut into his maw. She rapped on the glass.

Garth jumped so hard he hit his head on the roof of the car. His hand went immediately to his belt, fumbling with the strap on his holster.

"Garth! It's just me! Roni!" she shouted through the glass, preparing to dive for cover. Garth Spall had never shot anyone, but he was notoriously quick to wave his gun around—which was why police chief Grant Hoff rarely let him go out on his own.

Garth recognized Roni and relaxed. Roni opened the door and climbed into the squad car. "Hi! How's it going?"

He looked at her suspiciously.

Roni pulled out her notebook. "I'm writing an article about Bloodwater's finest. I was wondering if I could interview you. You know—straight from the mouths of the men on the front line? Since you're the youngest and most physically powerful member of the department, I thought I'd start with you."

Garth stared at her. He may have been thinking, but she didn't wait to find out.

"After all, you're the department's future. The police force is aging. Another ten years and you'll have Grant Hoff's job." She gave him her most sincere fake smile and pointed at his face. "You have icing on your chin."

Garth wiped his face with the back of his hand. "Chief Hoff says don't talk to reporters."

"I'm sure he wasn't talking about *me,*" Roni said. "I mean, it's just the high school newspaper."

"I don't know . . . "

"Hey!" Roni turned her attention to the computer mounted on the center console between them. "I bet you can find out all kinds of cool stuff on here. Am I on it?"

"You?"

"Yeah. Am I on your master criminal database?"

"I don't know. Have you committed any crimes recently?"

"Nothing serious," Roni said. "I bet if you know somebody's name and address and license number, you can find out all kinds of stuff." She reached toward the keyboard. Garth slapped her hand away.

"Ouch! Police brutality!"

Garth looked alarmed.

Roni laughed. "Just kidding. So, when you pull somebody over for speeding or something, do you look them up on the computer?"

"If I don't know them."

"How do you do it?"

"I just enter in their license number. It tells me if the car is stolen, and who it belongs to, and stuff like that. It's easy."

"Show me."

"First I have to pull somebody over."

"Can't you just make up a number? You know, so I get it right in my article."

"I don't know . . . "

"Let's pretend. This little green car goes screaming past you, a hundred miles an hour. You hit the siren and go after them—"

"Hot pursuit. We call it hot pursuit."

"Hot pursuit. Got it." Roni wrote it down in her notebook. "So you're catching up to them—"

"I'm calling it in on the radio, just in case it's, you know, like a bank robbery."

"Right." The last bank robbery in Bloodwater had taken

place before Roni was born. "Anyway, you pull them over, and—"

"I type in their license number."

As his hand moved toward the keyboard, Roni rattled off the license number of the Asian woman's car. Garth typed it in and waited. A few seconds later, he said, "Green Hyundai Sonata. Registered to Kyung-Soon Kim. St. Paul address." He turned the screen so Roni could see.

"Wow," she said. "That's amazing." She wrote down the name and address in her notebook.

"No criminal record," Garth said.

Roni smiled. "I wonder why she was in such a hurry."

"I didn't even know those Hyundais could go that fast," Garth Spall said.

22
an old friend

Brian's dad was waiting at the curb when class let out. Brian said good-bye in Korean to Molly, then ran down the steps to the car.

"How was your class today, son?" asked Mr. Bain.

"It was *choun*. That means 'good' in Korean—I think. How was your Mensa meeting?"

Mr. Bain laughed. "Like always—a room full of extremely intelligent, socially inept adults attempting to interact with one another. It's rather like being in a room full of extraterrestrials." He put the car in gear and pulled onto the street.

"What do you talk about?" Brian asked.

"Today we talked about intelligence in annelids."

Brian knew what annelids were—his dad had written several books about them. "You talked about *worms*?"

"Yes. It was my turn to deliver the weekly presentation." He frowned. "It was not as well received as I had hoped."

"Speaking of worms, I had squid for lunch," Brian said.

"Squid are not worms. Squid are mollusks, as are octopuses and oysters."

"Oh. Hey, Dad, is it possible that I have a twin?"

"Twin? Oh. I see. You are wondering about your doppelganger, the boy who was abducted."

"This girl from class says that she knows a kid who looks exactly like me."

"I suppose it's *possible* that you have a twin, but I think it's highly unlikely. As you know, you were a foundling. You were not more than a week or two old, and you were alone. I can't imagine why, if a woman had given birth to a set of twins, she would abandon one child and not the other."

"Do you trust the records they gave you?"

"The Korean adoption services are very precise and rigorous about such things, son. They would have no reason to deceive us."

"But if I *did* have a twin . . . "

"It would be quite a coincidence—especially if you were adopted separately—for you to both end up in the same part of America, don't you think?"

"I suppose. . . . Hey, you know that Korean coin I have?"

"The ten won piece. Yes."

"Where did I get it?"

"I don't know," said Mr. Bain. "You've had it as long as I can remember. I assume you got it from the Samuelses."

"Is it valuable?" Brian asked.

His father smiled. "In Seoul you might be able to buy a

small piece of candy with it." He turned off the highway onto a bumpy dirt road.

"Where are we going?"

"To see some old friends, Jack and Theresa Hanke. You've never met them."

"Is this the surprise?"

"I suppose it is." They followed the road for about a mile, cornfields on either side, then turned into a driveway that led to a small farm. Chickens scattered as they pulled up to the freshly painted white farmhouse. A gray-haired man wearing brown coveralls waved from the open doorway of the barn. Three orange cats, their tails held high, came trotting toward them.

Brian and his dad got out of the car. The rich, organic aroma of the farm swept over them. It was strong, but it smelled good. The banging of a screen door caught his attention. A woman stepped out from the house, accompanied by a small, pale-brown terrier. The dog ran straight up to Brian, sniffed his leg, then backed up a few steps and began barking and wagging his tail vigorously.

The man, Jack Hanke, let loose a laugh that sounded like someone banging on a steel barrel. "I think he remembers you, boy!"

The dog would not stop barking.

"Sniffer?" Brian said.

The dog was wagging his tail so hard his whole rear end was shaking. Jack Hanke laughed some more, and his wife,

Theresa, joined in. Brian looked at his father. Were those tears in his eyes? Must be his allergies acting up.

"What should I do?" Brian said.

Jack Hanke said, "Hold out your arms."

Brian held out his arms. Sniffer sprang through the air into his embrace.

If Brian didn't want to unravel the mystery of his own life, that was fine with Roni. She would do it herself. She would find out who Kyung-Soon Kim was, and why she was interested in Brian, and she would find out what the orange-haired lady wanted, and . . . and what? She slumped in her chair and stared at her computer. It just wasn't as much fun to solve a mystery without her sidekick.

Roni reread the articles she'd downloaded from the *Star Tribune*. There wasn't a lot of information. Then she noticed a quote from Vera Doblemun's mother:

"She wasn't the type of person to just run off like that. I can't believe she wouldn't at least have called us to let us know she was all right."

It did seem odd that Vera Doblemun wouldn't have called her parents. Had she contacted them since the article was written? Roni read the article again, then typed the names of Vera Doblemun's parents—Alexander and Marianne Kay—into her computer. A few seconds later she was looking at an address in Hastings, Minnesota.

Hastings was only fifteen miles away, but without Hillary,

it might as well have been on Pluto—unless she could talk her mom into letting her use the car.

"How are you feeling, son?" Mr. Bain asked.

Brian, scrunched down in the passenger seat of his dad's car, did not know how he was feeling.

"Brian?"

"I'm okay, I guess," Brian said.

"He's an old dog," said Mr. Bain. "It wouldn't be fair to him to take him off the farm. He's just as attached to Jack and Theresa as he was to you."

"I know. I didn't expect him to come with us. I just . . . It was weird is all. Seeing him again. I mean, for most of my life I thought Sniffer was just a dream."

"I'm sorry we had to give him away. You were so young, and I was working every day at the college back then, and your mother was working all day, too, and we just didn't think we could take good care of both you and Sniffer. Also, I'm allergic to dogs." He sneezed, as if to prove his point.

"I didn't forget him," Brian said.

"No, you didn't."

They pulled into their driveway. Brian got out of the car and went upstairs to his room. He got out his Korean coin and stared at it. He had the coin, and some fuzzy memories of the Samuelses, and now the renewed memory of his dog. Only Sniffer wasn't his dog anymore.

He thought about calling Roni to tell her about Sniffer, but decided not to. She would probably make some comment about how the dog being alive proved her whole stupid theory about his parents kidnapping him. Or maybe she would decide that the Hankes were his real parents, and he wasn't really Korean, but had been altered by a diabolical surgeon who had erased his memory and planned to use him to take over the world.

His mom knocked on his door and stuck her head in.

"Brian?"

"What?"

"You were asking about your adoption papers. I have them here if you'd like to look at them." She held out a large three-ring notebook.

"Okay." He took the notebook from his mother and put it on his desk.

"Your father and I are driving up to the Mall of America to shop for a new sofa. Would you like to come?"

"No, thanks."

"We'll probably have dinner up there and not be home until late. Will you be okay by yourself?"

"Two words, Mom. Pizza hotdish."

23
mrs. kay

Roni spent twenty minutes psyching herself up to ask Nick if she could use her car. It wouldn't be easy—Nick would question her about her destination, and she would have to lie. Then her mom would make her explore every possible alternative form of transportation, then she would lecture her on personal responsibility, and then, in all likelihood, she would say no.

Roni took a deep breath and marched into the living room, where Nick was stretched out on the sofa reading a mystery. Her mom liked to take time to relax after work—before making dinner or, more likely, ordering a pizza.

"Mom, can I use the car for an hour or so?" Roni asked, bracing herself for Nick's response.

"Sure," Nick said without looking up from her book.

"Really?" Roni couldn't believe her luck. Then she got nervous. What was her mother up to? She didn't usually just let her have the car like that. "What do I have to do?"

"Nothing. Although if you feel like picking up a roasted chicken from the grocery store, that would be nice."

"So . . . I can have the car?"

Her mom tipped down her book and gave Roni a look. "Yes, I said."

"Why are you giving in so easily?"

"You haven't been in trouble for a while. You're a good driver. Plus, I like to surprise you from time to time. Keeps you on your toes." Her mom turned back to the book.

"I won't be gone long."

Her mother didn't say anything.

Sixty seconds later, Roni was in the car and headed for Hastings.

Alexander and Marianne Kay lived in a large, expensive-looking house on the south side of Hastings. A brand-new Mercedes-Benz was parked in their driveway. Roni parked behind the Mercedes and sat in her car for a few minutes, getting her story ready. The front door opened and a woman with steely-gray hair and a bright pink housecoat leaned out and gave her a quizzical look. Roni waved and got out of the car. She gave the woman her best smile and trotted up the flagstone path to the front steps.

"Can I help you?" asked the woman.

"Are you Mrs. Kay?" Roni asked.

"I am. Are you selling cookies?"

Cookies? Roni did her best not to scowl. Since when did she look like a Girl Scout?

"Actually, I wanted to ask you about your daughter and your grandson," Roni said.

It was as if every muscle in Mrs. Kay's face went slack. The smile disappeared, and her eyes went dead.

Roni said, "I'm sorry. I guess it must still be hard for you."

"You have no idea," said Mrs. Kay, speaking slowly. "I suppose you are here to inquire about the reward."

"Reward? What reward?" Roni said.

Mrs. Kay regarded Roni suspiciously. "What exactly is it you want?" she asked.

"My name is P. Q. Delicata," Roni said. "I'm a reporter for the *Bloodwater Pump.*" Marianne Kay would not know that the *Pump* was just a high school newspaper.

"You seem quite young to be a reporter," said Mrs. Kay.

"I'm new."

"How nice for you," said Mrs. Kay. "I'm old."

Roni wasn't sure if she was supposed to laugh, so she just smiled.

"Do people really call you P. Q.?" Mrs. Kay asked.

"That's my byline," Roni said. "Most people just call me Roni. I'm working on a story about unsolved child abductions in Minnesota, and I was wondering if we could talk."

They stared at each other for a few seconds. Mrs. Kay opened the door wider. "Would you like to come in?"

24

strong boy

Brian stared at the notebook for a long time without opening it. His name, Brian Bain, was printed on the cover of the book in his mother's neat hand. He knew what he would find: *One-week-old baby found outside police station. Sent to America because nobody in Korea wanted him. Adopted by people who died. Dog given away. Adopted by Bruce and Annette Bain.* The notebook was about two inches thick. What else could be in there?

Finally, with a sense of dread, he opened it and began to read.

The first few pages were typewritten forms from the Eastern Child Welfare Society. He figured that was the name of the orphanage where the cops took him after he was dumped. To his surprise, they had given him a name at the orphanage: Sang-Ki. They had even typed the meaning of the name in English: Vigorous Benevolence. Reading further, he discovered that as a baby he'd had a good appetite, excellent bowel movements, and strong lungs. He supposed that meant he ate, pooped, and cried a lot. There were three pages about his health—probably so that whoever adopted him would be reassured that he wasn't going to get sick and die.

There were two pictures of him being held by a Korean woman—probably one of the workers at the orphanage—then several complicated forms from the Children's Home Society of Minnesota. That must be the adoption agency. Owen and Janice Samuels's signatures were at the bottom of the last page.

The next page was an article cut from the Minneapolis paper. The headline read, "Orphans Flight Brings New Families Together." The article was about a flight on which eleven Korean orphans traveled from Seoul to Minneapolis to meet their adoptive families for the first time. One photo was of a man cradling an Asian infant as a woman looked on. The man was identified as Owen Samuels. The woman was his wife.

They looked like nice people. Brian imagined the sound of the man laughing, and suddenly he saw both of them, sharp and clear in his memory. Blinking back tears, he turned the page.

There were several pages of photos of Brian's first three and a half years: Brian at a birthday party, Brian playing with Sniffer, Brian dressed up as Batman, and so on. Then came a yellowed newspaper article about the deaths of the Samuelses. Their car had hit an icy bridge over the Bloodwater River, spun out of control, and crashed through the rail into the water. Brian knew that bridge. He had walked across it. He had canoed beneath it.

The rest of the book documented his life after his current parents had adopted him. He paged through it slowly. The last item was a clipping from last week's *Bloodwater Clarion*—the photo of him holding the SS-XLR8.

Brian closed the notebook. He flopped onto his bed and tried to not think. But that was impossible. His parents were driving up to Bloomington, to the Mall of America. They could get run over by a semi or go flying off a bridge. Then where would he go? He knew it was stupid to think that way, but he couldn't help it.

The telephone rang, saving him from his thoughts. He rolled off the bed and answered the phone at his desk.

"Hello?"

"Greetings, Watson." It was Roni. "I'm calling from the road."

"Hey."

"I know you have lost every last ounce of curiosity, but I thought you might like to know the identity of the mysterious woman who has been watching you."

"The orange-haired lady?" Brian said.

"No. The one in the green car who was spying on you at the marina."

"I didn't see anybody spying on me."

"That's why it's called spying, Einstein."

Brian remembered the woman who had spoken to him just before he'd had his encounter with Mrs. Atkinson's rhododendron bush. "Was she Asian?"

"Yes!"

"Was she driving a green Hyundai?"

"Yes! You've seen her before?"

"Just once. What makes you think she was spying on me?"

"'Cause I saw her doing it."

"Okay, so who is she?"

"Her name is Kyung-Soon Kim. She lives in St. Paul."

"I've never heard of her."

"Isn't Kim a Korean name?"

"Yeah, but so what?"

"I don't know, but I do know why you've got all these people looking for you."

"Why?"

"You're worth a hundred thousand dollars."

"Is that all?"

"Seriously. I met with Vera Doblemun's mother. They're offering a one-hundred-thousand-dollar reward for the safe return of their daughter and their grandson, Bryce Doblemun."

"So actually I'm only worth fifty thousand," Brian said. "And only if I'm Bryce, which I'm not."

"I think the Asian woman, and the one with orange hair, and maybe some other people saw your picture in the paper and thought you were Bryce, so now they want to turn you in for the reward."

"Wow. That actually makes sense."

"It might explain why Lance Doblemun wanted to get his hands on you, too."

"So he could turn in his own adopted son to collect a reward from his in-laws?"

"He was eating *squirrels,*" Roni pointed out. "And a hundred thousand is a lot of money. In fact, I was thinking, how would anybody ever know you *weren't* really Bryce?"

"Wait a second—*you* want to turn me in for the reward?"

"I'd split it with you."

Brian was speechless.

Roni laughed. "Kidding!"

Brian said, "You know what, though? There might be a way we could collect that reward, if . . ."

"How?"

"I might have a lead on the *real* Bryce Doblemun. Can you come over here for dinner?"

"I'm supposed to pick up dinner for my mom."

"I'm making my new specialty. Pizza hotdish."

"Pizza hotdish? Sounds disgusting."

"It is. Are you in?"

"I'm in."

25

pizza soup

Roni handed her mom the roast chicken. "Mission accomplished."

"Great, I'm starved," said Nick. She started digging around in the refrigerator. "I think we've got some salad greens in here someplace."

Roni said, "Nick, what would you do if you all of a sudden had a hundred thousand dollars?"

"Pay off the house. Put some money away for your college education. Fly to Barbados."

"I like the Barbados part."

"Oh, I wouldn't take you." Nick smiled, rubbed Roni's head, and said, "Just kidding. I'd even buy you a new bathing suit."

"Could I get a thong?" Roni asked.

Nick laughed and began to set the table.

Roni said, "Just set it for one, Mom. I'm having dinner over at the Bains."

"Really?" Nick gave her daughter an irritated, slightly offended look. "No eating roast chicken together? No girl talk about what we're going to do with money we don't have?"

"I'm sorry, Mom," said Roni. She really did feel bad about it. "Brian invited me over for dinner and I couldn't say no."

Nick was standing with her arms crossed, giving her the gimlet eye.

"Roni, you know I trust you."

"You do?"

"I would ask you where you went with my car for almost two hours, but I'm afraid that if I did, you might feel like you had to lie to me."

Roni didn't say anything. It was true. To deny it would make the unspoken lie even worse.

Nick's shoulders sagged. "I was afraid of that."

For his second attempt at pizza hotdish, Brian decided to triple the amount of pepperoni and cheese, his two favorite pizza toppings. To balance it out, he added an extra can of chopped tomatoes. He thought it would be nice to have a crust, so before pouring the gloppy mixture of rigatoni, cheese, pepperoni, and tomatoes into the casserole, he lined the sides with crackers. Unfortunately, the crackers became dislodged and floated to the top.

Oh, well. He stuck the pan in the oven and set the timer. It would probably be edible.

Roni showed up just as Brian was pulling the hotdish from the oven.

"Smells like pizza," she said.

Brian looked at the soupy, bubbling concoction. It looked

weird—like tomato-and-cheese soup with soggy crackers floating on top.

"I think we better let it cool down," he said. "Maybe it'll solidify."

"Fine. While it's cooling, tell me what you learned about your doppelganger."

"Okay, but first I have to tell you something else. I found Sniffer!"

"Who's Sniffer?"

"My dog. I told you I remembered having a dog? Well, I did, and he's still alive, living on a farm up by Prescott. My dad took me to see him."

"Cool! Are they going to give him back to you?"

"I don't think so."

"Oh. I'm sorry."

"It's okay. Sniffer likes living on the farm." Brian got some plates out of the cupboard and put them on the table. "Tell me about this reward."

Roni told him how she'd found Vera Doblemun's parents' names from a newspaper article, and about getting their address off the Internet, and persuading her mom to let her use the car, and telling Mrs. Kay she was a reporter, and—

"What do you want to drink?" Brian asked, interrupting her.

"Red wine?"

Brian poured her a glass of cranberry juice and held it up to the light. "Close enough?"

"Perfect. Anyway, ten years ago, Mr. and Mrs. Kay offered a reward for finding their daughter and grandson, but all they got was a bunch of false leads. The reward is still good, though, even though they've pretty much given up hope."

"It seems weird that you didn't hear about this reward before," Brian said. "You'd think they'd have it posted on the Internet."

"I asked her about that. I guess there was a lot of publicity the first couple of years after Vera and Bryce disappeared, but now it's just on that missing-kids site, and they don't post rewards there. Anyway, I said, 'I interviewed Bryce's father a few days ago. I wonder why he didn't mention the reward.'

"Mrs. Kay got really upset then. She couldn't believe I'd talked to Lance Doblemun. 'That man is evil,' she told me. She doesn't believe her daughter abducted Bryce. She and her husband think something awful happened to both of them, and that Lance Doblemun had something to do with it."

Brian said, "I could believe it. He looked capable of anything."

Roni sat down at the table and propped her chin on her hands. "Your turn. What did you find out about Bryce Doblemun?"

"I went to my Korean Culture class this morning," Brian said. "I know how to say *squid* in Korean now . . ."

"Please don't," Roni said.

". . . and I met a girl who says she knows a kid who looks exactly like me."

26

louella

Brian grinned as he set the casserole on the table.

"Ta-da," he said. "Pizza hotdish."

"I'm not eating a bite until you tell me more about this doppelganger," Roni said.

"All in good time, Holmes." Brian scooped servings of hotdish onto their plates. It was a little loose. "Maybe we should have used bowls," he said.

"It does look a bit like, um, pizza soup. What are those soggy white squares on top?"

"That's the crust."

"Hmm."

They sat down, but neither of them made a move to eat.

"I'm waiting," Roni said.

"It might be nothing," Brian said. "But a girl in my Korean class thought she knew me. She said I was a dead ringer for this kid she met at the Korean Cultural Center in St. Paul."

"A kid named Bryce?"

"A kid named Dak-Ho. His English name is Billy. Only

she didn't know exactly where he lived. But I bet if we went to the Korean Cultural Center we could—"

He was interrupted by the doorbell.

"I wonder who that is," he said.

Roni went to the window and peeked out past the blinds.

"Uh-oh," she said.

"What? Who is it?" Brian ran to the window.

"Don't let her see you!" Roni said. The woman standing on the front steps was nearly six feet tall, a good three hundred pounds, about sixty years old, with an imperious nose, a slash of red lipstick, jeweled eyeglasses, and an oversize brocade purse. But her most prominent feature was a cloud of curly, unnaturally bright orange hair.

"She's the woman I saw at the library," Roni said. The woman rang the doorbell again, this time holding it down for several seconds.

"What do you think we should do?" Brian asked.

"I'm going to talk to her," Roni said. "Stay out of sight."

The woman was pressing the doorbell for the third time. Roni ran to the front door, took a deep breath, and opened it. She and the woman stared at each other for about six heartbeats. Then the woman said, "I'm looking for a young man named Brian Bain."

"Brian?" Roni put on her puzzled face.

"Young lady, I know the boy lives here. I have it on good authority."

"Really? From who?"

"If you must know, I spoke with several persons, including your next-door neighbor. Are you his sister?"

"Cousin," Roni said. "Why are you looking for Brian?"

The woman regarded Roni the way she might look at a stain on a carpet. For a moment, Roni thought the woman was going to shove her aside and ransack the house, but she seemed to get control of herself and said, "It is a personal matter, but I can tell you this. There is a great deal of money involved, and your cousin might well benefit."

"Who are you?" Roni asked.

"My name is Louella Doblemun," the woman said.

"Doblemun? Are you by any chance related to *Lance* Doblemun?"

Louella Doblemun's eyes bulged and her red lips fell open. "How do you know my son?" she asked.

"Why are you looking for Brian?" Roni countered.

"Young lady—"

"Look, he's not here. Brian and his father went to Tierra del Fuego to study penguins."

"Oh. Well." Mrs. Doblemun leaned forward and looked suspiciously past Roni into the house.

"Do you want to leave a message?"

The woman ignored Roni's question. "Tell me, the boy's mother, is she a small woman, blue eyes, with a pinched face and a whiny voice?"

Brian's mother looked nothing like that at all. Mrs.

Doblemun must have been describing Vera Doblemun, her daughter-in-law.

"That doesn't sound like her," Roni said. Looking past Louella Doblemun, she noticed a big silver car with tinted windows parked on the street. She could see the shape of a man sitting in the passenger seat, but she couldn't make him out clearly.

Mrs. Doblemun asked, "When will they be back from—where did you say?"

"Tierra del Fuego."

"Hmph! When do you expect them to return?"

"Not for another month," Roni said.

Once again, the woman squared her shoulders as if she were about to charge into the house. Roni braced herself. "You do know that Mrs. Bain is a policewoman, right?" she said quickly.

Louella Doblemun's shoulders sagged. "I see. Well, then. We'll be back." She turned and lumbered back to her car. Roni closed the door and ran back toward the kitchen, almost crashing into Brian, who had been listening from around the corner.

"Did you see who was in the car with her?" he asked.

"I couldn't make him out, but I bet I could guess."

"Well, I could see him from the kitchen window. It was—"

Roni finished his sentence for him. "Lance Doblemun."

27

crazy mirror

"So Lance Doblemun and his mother think you're Bryce, and they're both way scary, and the real Bryce is living in St. Paul, and—"

"Wait a second—I just said a kid who *looks* like me lives in St. Paul."

"A kid who *could* be Bryce Doblemun lives in St. Paul. I think we should check it out."

Brian got up from the table and went to the window. Louella Doblemun's car was still parked in front of the house. "What are they *doing* out there?"

"Probably figuring out how to capture you."

"Shut *up*."

"I don't think she believed me that you were in Tierra del Fuego."

"What if they sit out there forever? We'll never be able to leave."

"We won't starve. We've got pizza soup."

Brian returned to the table and stared down at his plate. He had been able to eat only a few bites. Roni had stopped at one.

"The first time I made it, it was pretty good," he said.

"Maybe if you hadn't put so much . . . I don't know . . . *everything* in it."

"I guess I'm kind of like my dad," Brian said. He went to look out the window again. "Hey, they're leaving."

"Good. Tell you what. It's only seven o'clock. We could drive up to St. Paul and check out the Korean Center. Maybe somebody there will recognize you—I mean *him*—and tell us where he lives. We could be home in a couple of hours."

"Sure, if we had a car."

"Maybe it's time to call in the reserves," Roni said.

"We have reserves?"

"I can't believe I let you talk me into this," Darwin Dipstick muttered as he pulled out onto the highway in his tow truck. Roni and Brian were riding on the seat beside him.

"How many hours did you say it would take to clean up your junkyard?" Roni asked. She had promised Darwin that she and Brian would help him clean up his junkyard if he would give them a ride up to St. Paul. She also got him to promise to fix Hillary's axle.

"It's not a junkyard. Those are rare and valuable auto parts."

"Well, Brian and I will be sure to treat them like precious gems as we dig them out of the weeds and throw them into neat, highly organized piles."

"Are there any *snakes* there?" Brian asked.

"I got this bull snake living under the fifty-four Ford

chassis," Darwin said. "Maybe a few garter snakes back there, too."

Roni groaned. What had she gotten herself into?

Brian said, "Got any tunes in this truck?"

Darwin pressed a button on the stereo and the cab of the truck exploded with the raucous 1970s rock 'n' roll of Lynyrd Skynyrd.

"That's what I'm talkin' 'bout!" Brian shouted over the din. Darwin grinned. Outnumbered, Roni sank lower in the front seat and braced herself for an hour of high-volume dinosaur rock.

By the time they hit St. Paul, Roni figured she'd lost about 10 percent of her hearing.

"Where is this place?" Darwin asked, turning down the volume slightly.

Roni pretended she couldn't hear him. *"What?"*

Darwin turned the stereo off and repeated his question.

Roni, looking at the map, said, "Get off at the Snelling Avenue exit and turn right. It's just a couple of miles."

Darwin exited the freeway.

"More tunes!" Brian yelled.

"No more tunes!" Roni said. "My ears are toast."

Darwin laughed.

Roni watched the street signs go by. Without the map she'd be completely lost. St. Paul was not exactly New York City, but compared with Bloodwater it was enormous. Roni read the street signs as they drove up Snelling Avenue, checking their progress on the map.

"Wait! Stop! Pull over!" she said.

Darwin pulled over to the curb. "What? Are we there?"

"We just passed Blair Avenue!"

"So? I thought you said this place was on Snelling."

Roni turned to look at Brian. "The woman in the green car lives on Blair."

"What woman?" Darwin said.

"We have to check her out," Roni said.

Darwin objected. "Hey, I said I'd take you to this Korean joint. You didn't say anything about going visiting."

"Just a drive-by," Roni said. She pulled out her notebook. "Thirty-seven twenty Blair Avenue. That can't be too far."

Darwin rolled his eyes and said something under his breath, then put the tow truck in gear and made a U-turn. Moments later, they were driving down Blair Avenue, searching for number 3720. It was starting to get dark, and the addresses were hard to see.

"There, that white house," said Roni, pointing at a small two-story house on the left side of the street.

"You can read the address from here?" Darwin said.

"I recognize the car out front. Slow down."

The house itself was perfectly ordinary looking, with white siding, a little flower garden, and a neatly trimmed lawn. A long-haired kid sat on the front steps under the porch light adjusting the wheels of a skateboard.

The kid looked up and Brian saw his face.

There are moments when the world twists upside down, when you can't believe what you're seeing, when you feel like you're in free fall without a parachute and everything you think you know makes no sense at all. Brian was having one of those moments.

The kid sitting on the steps had long black hair and was wearing a baseball cap backward. He had a round face, dusky-gold skin, dark eyes, and an earring in his left ear. Nothing unusual in all that—except that his face was Brian's face. Exactly. Identical.

Feeling as if he were in a dream, Brian climbed out of the tow truck and crossed the street. The kid with the skateboard watched him approach. When he was about five feet away, Brian halted and stared.

It was like looking at himself in a crazy mirror, one that gave him long hair and an earring. He liked the long hair. He loved the earring.

The kid gave a slight laugh and said, "Hey, bro. What's up?"

28

dak-ho

Roni had never thought about it before, but give Brian an earring and get him to grow his hair long, and he had cute potential. The kid with the skateboard looked like a hipper, more sophisticated version of Brian. She followed Brian up the walk and heard him say, "Dak-Ho?"

The long-haired version of Brian laughed and said, "Dude, that's my Korean name."

"I'm Brian," said Brian.

"I know who you are, bro."

"You do?"

"Sure."

Darwin, standing just behind Roni, asked, "Who's the clone?"

"That's what we're here to find out." She stepped up beside Brian. Might as well cut to the chase. "Are you Bryce Doblemun?" she asked.

The kid gave Roni a long, suspicious look.

"Who are you?" he asked.

"Roni Delicata."

"She's my friend," Brian said.

"What about him?" the kid said, looking at Darwin.

"That's Darwin. He gave us a ride up here. He's okay."

The kid thought for a moment, then shrugged. "My name is Billy Kim," he said. "I'm your twin bro, bro."

Brian stood and stared, speechless.

"You aren't Bryce Doblemun?" Roni said.

"Never heard of him," said Billy Kim.

"How do you know you two are brothers?" Roni asked.

"My mom told me. Besides—just look at us!"

"Isn't your mom Vera Doblemun?"

"I told you, I don't know any Doblemuns."

"Then who is your mom?" Roni asked.

Billy looked at Brian. "Is she always so pushy?"

"Yep," Brian said. "And she never stops asking questions until she gets the answers."

"My mom is my mom," Billy said to Roni. "Her name is Kyung-Soon."

"Kyung-Soon is your adoptive mom?" Roni asked.

"No, she's my real mom." He looked at Brian. "I mean, *our* real mom."

This situation was getting weirder by the moment. "You mean your real-biological-from-Korea mom?"

Billy nodded.

Roni looked over at Brian. He looked pale, as if he were about to topple over.

"My first mom?" Brian finally whispered.

"*Our* mom," Billy reminded him.

"What's going on here?" Darwin asked. "You two guys

are brothers, but you don't know each other, and . . . how many moms do you *have,* anyway?"

"I need to sit down," Brian said. He didn't even bother to walk over to the front steps, but just sank down onto the concrete walkway.

Billy said, "You didn't know about me, did you?"

Brian shook his head.

"We lost you. My mom said you were taken from her in Korea. She found out you'd been adopted by a family here in Minnesota. When I was three years old, we moved here to be closer to you, but when she found you, you were living with some people she said were really nice, and you seemed happy. But then the people who adopted you were killed, and we lost track of you until a couple of weeks ago, when my mom saw you in the paper."

"The paper-airplane picture?"

"Yeah. Cool airplane. I'd like to know how to fold it."

"I didn't know I had a twin."

Billy nodded. "It must be kind of a shock."

"A tidal wave."

"Are you, like, really smart?"

Brian looked up at the sky. "I skipped a grade," he said.

"I can speak Korean," Billy said.

"I can say *good morning* and *thank you,* but not very well."

"I'll teach you."

Roni said, "Hey, guys, focus. What about Bryce Doblemun?"

"What is it with her and this Doblemun kid?" Billy asked Brian.

Brian shrugged. "She's Roni."

Brian and Billy had met only two minutes ago, and already they were acting like they'd known each other their entire lives.

Roni said, "If you aren't Bryce Doblemun, then why is your picture on the missing-kids website?"

"What're you talking about? I've never been missing."

Brian said, "Roni, don't you get it? Bryce Doblemun was just some kid who maybe looked a little bit like me and Billy. It's a coincidence."

"I don't believe in coincidences," Roni said. "I want to talk to your mom. Is she home?"

"She's taking a nap," Billy said.

Brian said, "Roni . . . "

"Can you wake her up?" Roni asked.

"Roni!" Brian was pointing toward the street.

Roni turned and saw a long silver car roll up behind Darwin's tow truck, right beneath a streetlamp. As she watched, the passenger door opened and a tall, thin, bearded man stepped out.

Lance Doblemun.

29

rope-a-dope

Louella Doblemun got out of the driver's side of the Cadillac. "Bryce! We've come to take you home, baby," she shouted. She lumbered across the street, holding her handbag as if it were a weapon. Her son followed close behind her.

"Now what?" Darwin said to no one in particular.

"That's far enough," said Roni as the Doblemuns reached the sidewalk. "This is private property."

Lance Doblemun and his mother stopped. Mrs. Doblemun pointed a finger at Brian and said, "Vera never should have stolen you away, young man. It's time to return to your real family."

"Who's Vera?" Billy asked.

"Who's *anybody*?" said Darwin, looking very confused.

"What are you doing here?" Roni asked the two Doblemuns.

Lance Doblemun said, "Dogged you all the way from Bloodwater, missy. You never noticed us. Big old tow truck like that, we just followed the smoke." He grinned at Darwin. "Lost you for a few minutes after you pulled that tricky turnaround back on Snelling, but not for long!"

Looking at Brian, he said, "Come on, Bryce, let's get you home." He took a step forward.

"If you take one more step, we're calling the police," Roni said.

"And my name isn't Bryce, it's Brian. There are no Bryces here."

Lance and his mother finally noticed Billy. They looked back and forth between the two boys, more confused with each passing second.

"Who are *you*?" Mrs. Doblemun asked Billy.

"Who are *you*?" Billy shot back.

"I am your grandmother!" She looked from Brian to Billy. "Or *his* grandmother!"

"*Our* grandmothers are Korean," Billy said.

Roni could have sworn she heard Lance Doblemun snarl, an evil, low-down sound that scared her to her bones. He looked as if he were about to snap.

"One of you has got to be him," said Lance, taking another step toward Brian and Billy.

Roni moved to put herself between Lance and Brian. "Just because you drove away your wife and son doesn't mean you can go grabbing every kid you think resembles him."

Lance seemed to really notice her for the first time. "You! You're the one who made me wreck my truck!"

"And you lied to me," Mrs. Doblemun said. "Tierra del Fuego indeed!"

Roni said, "You don't really want Bryce back at all—you just want to collect the reward."

"This has nothing to do with money," Mrs. Doblemun said.

"Money's nice, though," Lance said. He lunged forward, shoving Roni aside with one arm. Roni fell to the grass, but she saw what happened next—Billy kicked his skateboard toward the charging Lance Doblemun. The board caught Lance in the shin and he went down with an anguished howl.

Mrs. Doblemun entered the fray, swinging her purse like a club. Darwin, in a state of utter bewilderment, took the whirling purse full in the face and went down like a sack of beans.

Billy yelled, "Come on!" and took off running, with Brian close behind. They disappeared around the corner of the house. Lance Doblemun scrambled to his feet and took off in pursuit. Mrs. Doblemun, satisfied that Darwin was out of commission, started after them. Roni grabbed Billy's skateboard and sent it rolling on an interception course. Louella Doblemun's left foot came down on the board. Her ankle twisted, her feet flew out from under her, and she landed with an earth-shaking *thump* flat on her back.

A few seconds later, Roni heard Brian's voice from the other side of the house.

"Roni! Help! Come quick!"

When Billy and Brian took off running, Billy had seemed to understand immediately that Lance Doblemun was a threat, and that they couldn't afford to let him catch either of them.

"Follow me," he said over his shoulder. "I've got an idea."

It was almost dark, that time of night when the color leaves the world and the shadows get confusing. Billy was running flat-out—it was all Brian could do to keep up with him. He had to trust that Billy knew the territory—it was so dark it was hard to see where they were going. They ran through the neighbor's backyard, jumped a low fence, and tore down the alley behind the houses. Lance was on their tail, not forty feet behind them. For an old guy, he was *fast*.

Billy made a hard right turn through an open gate. He zigged around a bush, then zagged around a window well on the side of a house. Brian wasn't sure, but it seemed like they were running in a circle and were now heading back to Billy's. He risked a quick glance over his shoulder. Lance was only about ten feet behind them. He could hear the man's ragged breathing.

"Faster," he yelled.

Billy put on a burst of speed across a yard that looked to Brian like it ended at a six-foot-tall fence. Brian sensed that Lance was a millisecond away from grabbing him when he heard a strangled squawk, followed by the thump of a body hitting the earth.

Billy and Brian skidded to a stop just before hitting the fence. Behind them, Lance Doblemun was writhing on the ground, clutching his throat and making noises that sounded like *aak* and *ulg*.

Brian immediately saw what had happened. Lance

Doblemun had been clotheslined. Literally. Billy had led them racing across his backyard in the near-darkness, knowing that a clothesline was stretched across it, and knowing that the line was just high enough for him and Brian to run beneath. In other words, at the exact height of Lance Doblemun's neck.

"Kuh. Uh. Erk!" Lance seemed to be saying, his eyes rolling.

Horrified, Brian wondered if Lance Doblemun was dying. Could he have crushed his windpipe?

Billy was pulling the clothesline down. "Help me," he said. "I don't want to take any chances with him."

Brian had once watched a rodeo on TV, and what he was seeing reminded him of the calf-roping event where the cowboys lassoed the calves and tied them up. Billy whipped the cord around Lance's ankles, and tied it.

Lance Doblemun, realizing what was happening, tried to sit up and grab Billy. Brian shouted to Roni for help, then ran behind Lance and grabbed a hank of his hair. He pulled back on it as hard as he could. Lance let out a yell and reached back, trying to grab Brian.

"Sit on him," Billy yelled, still wrestling with Lance's feet.

Brian threw himself across Lance Doblemun's chest. The man twisted and turned beneath him, trying to buck him off. For a second, Brian thought that he and Billy might be able to control him—but then he felt Lance Doblemun's fingers wrap around his throat and start to squeeze.

30

kyung-soon

Roni ran around the house toward the sound of Brian's voice. She found the three of them—Lance, Brian, and Billy—rolling on the ground fighting. She stopped, trying to make sense of the tangle of arms and legs. Billy was hanging on to Lance's legs. Brian was on top of his chest, but the man had his hands locked around Brian's throat.

Without thinking, Roni threw herself onto the pile. She felt her knee sink into Lance's gut and heard the *whuff* of air exploding from his lungs. His hands released Brian's neck. Brian fell backward, and Lance Doblemun began making a new sound—the *heeek heeek heeek* of someone who had the wind knocked out of him.

"Here," Billy said. He handed her the clothesline. Roni thought for a split second, then threw the end of the clothesline out across the yard. She and Billy quickly rolled the gasping man over the stretched-out cord so that it wrapped several times around his body, pinning his arms to his sides. Brian, seeing what they were doing, had pulled down a second clothesline. A few seconds later, Lance was wrapped up like a fly in a spider's web.

"Ha," said Billy, climbing to his feet. "Spider-Man couldn't have done better."

"Dak-Ho?" A new voice came from the side of the house. A small, dark-haired woman stepped into the backyard. "Dak-Ho? Who are these people? And what are you—oh!" She stopped, seeing the man on the ground. For about three seconds, nobody moved or said anything.

Billy was the first to speak.

"Hi, Mom," he said.

Brian recognized her at once. This was the same woman who had warned him about skateboarding down the hill in Bloodwater. But this time he knew, deep in his heart, without a trace of doubt, that he was looking at the woman who had given birth to him.

She did not speak. Her eyes were fixed on the man on the ground. Lance Doblemun, now helpless, glared back at her, his jaw pulsing.

Billy said to Brian, "This is our mom, Kyung-Soon."

The woman's eyes went to Brian, and then Roni, then back to Lance Doblemun.

"This man, he is very dangerous," she said.

"You know him?" Billy said.

Kyung-Soon sat down on the back steps, looking small and frightened. She began to rock back and forth, wringing her hands.

"Mom? Are you okay?"

Kyung-Soon shook her head. Looking from Billy to

Brian, she said, "There are things I must tell you. Both of you."

Roni, looking around nervously, said, "What about Mrs. Doblemun?"

As she spoke, Louella Doblemun came limping around the corner of the house, wincing with pain every time she put weight on her right foot. When she saw Lance lying on the ground, she let out a screech.

"What have you done to my son?" She hobbled quickly to him and sank to her knees. "Lance, baby, what have they done to you?"

"Just untie me," he said.

Mrs. Doblemun started to tug at the ropes. Kyung-Soon's voice rang out, sharp and clear and much louder than anyone expected.

"Do not untie him."

Mrs. Doblemun looked at Kyung-Soon, startled.

"Who are *you*?" she asked.

"I am Kyung-Soon Kim. I am mother to these boys, and you will listen to me. All of you."

"I'm not listening to anybody until you untie my son!"

"Yes, you will—if you ever want to know what really happened to Vera Doblemun and your grandson Bryce."

That had an effect on Mrs. Doblemun. "What do *you* know?" she asked.

"I know *everything*," said Kyung-Soon.

31

blood and tea

"This had better be good," said Mrs. Doblemun.

Kyung-Soon shook her head. "It is not good. Nothing about it is good." She gave Lance a long, measuring look, then said to Billy, "Is he well tied?"

"I think so," Billy said.

Kyung-Soon stood up. "Then let us go inside where we do not have to look at him." To Mrs. Doblemun, she said, "If you wish to know the truth about my son—and yours—you will come inside and listen."

Mrs. Doblemun slowly stood up.

"You can't just leave me here!" Lance said.

Just then, Darwin appeared, rubbing his head and looking a bit discombobulated. "What's going on?" he said. "What happened?" Seeing Mrs. Doblemun, he stopped and backed up a step. She scowled at him.

Roni said, "Darwin, would you stay out here and keep an eye on him?" She pointed at Lance.

"Huh?"

"Just for a few minutes, while we go inside and talk?"

After pointing out the time, and the long drive ahead of

them, Darwin agreed, grudgingly, and settled into the chaise longue by the back door.

As they trooped into the house, Roni was already writing her story in her head, thinking she might be able to sell it to *The New York Times,* or failing that, the *Bloodwater Clarion.* What a story! Korean twins separated at birth and now reunited halfway around the world, a purse-swinging grandmother, a hundred-thousand-dollar reward, and an evil adoptive father trussed up like lunch for a giant spider.

As soon as they got inside, Kyung-Soon put a pot of water on for tea. "Large news should always have tea," she explained, placing a large teapot on the kitchen table where Roni, Billy, and Brian were sitting.

Mrs. Doblemun limped into the living room and collapsed on the sofa, positioning herself so she could see into the kitchen through the doorway. "I think I need a doctor," she said. Her ankle was swelling visibly. "That child—" She glared at Roni. "That child attacked me with a skateboard."

Kyung-Soon took a bag of frozen peas from the freezer and put it on Mrs. Doblemun's injured ankle. "Time for the doctor later," she said. She poured hot water into the teapot. "Time now to tell my story. My story of two sons, and my father, and my family's shame."

She bowed her head as if in prayer. Then she started to talk again in her low, slow voice. "I was very young when I became pregnant, only a girl, too young to know it could even happen. I had two boys. Twins. My father was very angry. My mother cried and cried. But I was happy. I had two beautiful sons. Then one night my babies disappeared. My father had taken them away. Later, I found out that he had split them up. He thought twins could not find a good home together, because who would want to adopt two children at once? One boy he left on the steps of the police station in Taegu City. The other he left at a hospital in Kyongsan. They ended up being sent to the same orphanage, but no one there knew they were brothers. A few months later, they flew to America, both on the same airplane, to live with different families here in Minnesota."

She poured the tea into five small ceramic tea bowls. "I screamed, I cried, I was furious at my father. I swore that one day I would find my children. I worked as hard as I could and saved money, hiding it from my father. I learned English. Three years later, I came to America. I hired a private detective, like the famous Sherlock Holmes."

Roni and Brian looked at each other.

"I wanted to know, at least, that they were okay," Kyung-Soon continued. "I knew I could never have them back, because the laws in this country would never allow it, but I had to know that they were with good families. Safe. Happy. My twin boys.

"After many months and much money, the detective found them, both in Minnesota." She looked at Brian. "You were living in a place called Cannon Falls, with good parents. I could see that they loved you. I was sad that I could not hold you in my arms, but you were safe and happy."

Brian was glad to hear that Kyung-Soon had liked the Samuelses.

"I had a dog," he said.

"Yes, I saw the dog. I left a Korean coin in his doghouse, for luck. Did you find it?"

"Yes! I still have it. A ten won piece. My dad says—ouch!" Roni had kicked him under the table. She wanted him to shut up, but it was his story, too. He kicked her back.

Kyung-Soon continued. "Different story with Dak-Ho. Billy. They called him Bryce. He was with the Doblemuns, and they fought. I would see them fighting. They fought every day, and the child cried in the night. I worried. I kept watch. I did not know what else to do.

"At last I had found them, two small boys of my own heart, but one was living in a house of unhappiness. One night I was watching. I crept up to the house, very quiet, and looked in the window. Dak-Ho was sitting with his back to me, watching the television.

"The woman was cleaning the table. The man had a bottle of beer in his hand. Suddenly he started yelling. I did not know the words—my English was not so good back then—but he was very angry. I wished my small boy did not live with this loud man.

"I could only see the dark back of his head, Dak-Ho. Very quiet. Not moving. I wished I could see his face. I wished I could touch his hair. I wished I could tell him he was my small boy and my love is as large as the ocean.

"The man yells again. The woman throws a plate at him.

He catches it and slams it down on the floor, very hard. Pieces fly. He is also coming apart. His hands fly out. One hits her in the face. She tries to get away, but he grabs her and throws her, and her head hits the edge of the table, and she falls broken to the floor.

"There is much blood."

Brian looked over at Billy, who was sitting very still, listening. Brian could tell he had never heard this story before.

Kyung-Soon reached over and touched Billy's hair. "Dak-Ho sat so very quiet. What a good boy he was. I wanted to run in and take him away, to make him safe, but the man walked over and lifted him and carried him up the stairs. A few minutes later he came back down the stairs, and he was alone.

"The woman had not moved. Her eyes were half open, not blinking, staring at her own blood dark on the floor. The man knelt down beside her. He knelt for a long time. I watched from the window, thinking of my small boy in the dark upstairs.

"Suddenly the man stood up. He stepped over the woman. I heard him open the door on the back of the house and go outside. Then I saw Dak-Ho come down the stairs. He went to the woman. His eyes were wide and open. He touched the blood with his little finger. He touched her light hair, so different from his."

Kyung-Soon began to weep. "I tried the door by the window, but it would not open. Then the man came back inside, and the small boy ran up the stairs. I could do nothing. I waited.

"The man closed the woman's eyes with his fingers. The eyes stayed closed. That was when I knew that those eyes would never open again."

A gasp came from the living room. Brian looked to see Mrs. Doblemun sitting up, eyes wide. "You are lying," she said in a broken voice. "Tell me you are lying."

Kyung-Soon shook her head and said, "I am sorry. I am sorry for your son. For you. For all of us. Your son is a murderer."

32

ki-nam

Roni saw Louella Doblemun's face crumple. The woman, so frightening and formidable half an hour ago, seemed to collapse in on herself. She began to sob. Roni actually felt sorry for her. What could it be like to discover that one's own son is a murderer?

"Lance Doblemun dug a hole in his backyard, very deep," said Kyung-Soon. "I watched him. And when he dragged his wife outside and put her in the hole, I climbed into the house through a window and I took Dak-Ho away with me.

"That was ten years ago. I had made friends here in St. Paul. They helped me. But I did not tell what I saw, because I was afraid the police would take Dak-Ho away from me. After a few weeks I went back to the place where Dak-Ho had lived. All that was left was a burnt bottom of house. I knew where the woman was buried, but I was afraid.

"I got a job teaching Korean, and Dak-Ho forgot all about that house of death and sorrow, and he grew tall and strong and happy. I gave him a new name. Billy. Billy Kim."

"So you never told the police what you saw?" Roni asked.

Kyung-Soon shook her head. "I was afraid if I came forward they would take Dak-Ho. He is not legally my son."

"But he *is* your son," Roni said.

"No, he's not." Louella Doblemun had recovered from her shock and was sitting up on the couch, looking entirely too much like her old self. "Bryce is my grandson. He belongs with his adoptive family."

"I'm not going anywhere with you," said Billy.

Mrs. Doblemun raised one painted eyebrow. "Oh, really? When I call the police, they'll return you to your rightful parent. Or, since my son may have legal troubles of his own, I will no doubt become your legal guardian."

Roni said, "You don't even *want* Billy—you just want to collect the reward."

Mrs. Doblemun shrugged. "Since the Kays have been so kind as to offer, I would not turn the money down. Now, come along, Bryce. Help your grandmother out to her car." She tried to stand, but gasped in pain when she tried to put weight on her ankle. She fell back onto the couch.

"My son is going nowhere with you," said Kyung-Soon. "Neither of them."

"The authorities may disagree with you," Mrs. Doblemun said. "I plan to collect both the boy *and* the reward."

"I'm confused all over again," Billy said. "What reward? Who are the Kays?"

"That does it," said Brian, pushing back his chair. He went to the phone by the refrigerator and dialed a number.

"Who are you calling?" Kyung-Soon asked.

"My other mother," Brian said.

Brian, Roni, and Kyung-Soon all gathered around the speakerphone in the kitchen and talked to Brian's mom, giving her the whole story. Even Louella Doblemun got into the act, screeching from her perch on the couch that no matter what her son had done, Bryce was her legal grandson, and that her poor son Lance was probably innocent anyway, and that she had a lawyer who would make shredded wheat out of anyone who tried to stop her.

Brian imagined his mother rolling her eyes and holding the phone away from her ear.

Although she said it was against her better judgment, Mrs. Bain agreed with Kyung-Soon's request not to call the St. Paul police immediately—at least not until she could get there to assess the situation. She also persuaded Louella Doblemun to sit tight for the time being. Not that Mrs. Doblemun had any choice—her ankle had swollen to the size of a cantaloupe. Brian's mom promised to straighten everything out once she got there. She also informed Brian that he should prepare himself to be grounded for all eternity.

"I'll be there in about forty minutes," she said, and hung up.

Billy looked at Brian. "Grounded for all eternity?" he said.

"It was worth it," Brian said. He looked at Kyung-Soon. "Do I have a Korean name?" he asked.

Kyung-Soon smiled. "You are Ki-Nam," she said. "It means 'strong boy.' I named you well."

"My American name—Brian—that means 'strong,' too," Brian said.

"Tell me about this reward," Billy said.

Brian and Roni told him about Vera Doblemun's parents, Alexander and Marianne Kay. "Do you remember them at all?" Brian asked.

Billy shook his head. "I was really little. I don't remember anything." He got up and went to the back door and looked out at Lance Doblemun. "I don't remember *him* at all."

Lance Doblemun, still securely bound, glared up at them. Darwin was stretched out on the chaise, snoring.

"I bet you blocked it out," Roni said. "It must have been awful."

"You know, if anybody turns me in for the reward, I might not be able to stay with my mom. She might get in trouble for taking me away. And for not reporting the murder."

"I know," Brian said, "but I think my mom—my adoptive mom—can help."

"She's really a cop?"

"Yep."

Kyung-Soon called to Billy from the kitchen. He went back inside and talked with his mother in Korean for a few minutes, then turned to Brian and said, "Could you guys wait out in the backyard? My mom and I need a few minutes."

"Wait—I have one question," Brian said. "When is our real birthday?"

Billy laughed, and then told him.

"Wow," Brian said. "I'm nine days older than I thought!"

Louella Doblemun was not thrilled about getting up off the sofa, but with Darwin's help they were able to move her onto the chaise longue outside.

Brian and Roni sat on the steps. They could hear movement and occasional bursts of rapid Korean from inside the house.

"What are they doing in there?" Roni said.

"I don't know," Brian said. "My mom will be here soon, and she'll know what to do."

"Would somebody *please* tell me what's going on?" Darwin said.

Roni took pity on him and explained the situation, with frequent corrections and embellishments from Brian. Mrs. Doblemun lay on the chaise, rolling her eyes, making *tch* sounds, putting her hands over her ears as Roni described what Kyung-Soon had seen the night she abducted Billy. Lance, meanwhile, stared at each of them in turn with an expression of hatred and despair.

When Roni had finished her story, they sat in silence. The sounds from inside the house had ceased, and all they heard was the chittering of crickets and the faint rush of distant traffic. After a minute or two, Roni said, "It's awfully quiet in there."

Brian had a thought. He jumped up and opened the back door.

"Hello?" he called out.

No answer.

He raised his voice. "Billy?"

Nothing. He entered the house and went from room to room. He ran up the stairs and looked into the bedrooms. No Billy. No Kyung-Soon. He ran back downstairs and out the front door.

Kyung-Soon's car was gone.

33

two families

Two days later, as Roni was rereading *The Hound of the Baskervilles,* her favorite Sherlock Holmes story, she heard the slap of the newspaper hitting the front steps. She ran downstairs and searched until she found the paper under the juniper bush. She opened the paper and saw the article immediately, right on the front page.

PEPIN MAN CONFESSES TO DECADE-OLD KILLING

Pepin, Wisconsin, resident Lawrence Doblemun was arrested by St. Paul Police Friday and charged in the death of his wife, Vera Doblemun. According to police, Mr. Doblemun confessed to the ten-year-old murder.

Mrs. Doblemun's body was recovered late Thursday from a grave in the backyard of the Doblemuns's former home, which burned to the ground shortly after Mrs. Doblemun and the couple's three-year-old son, Bryce, disappeared.

> The murder was brought to light when Bloodwater teens Brian Bain and Roni Delicata followed up on a lead from a picture of Bryce Doblemun that had been posted online.
>
> Bryce Doblemun, 13, remains missing, but the investigation revealed that he was alive and well as of last Thursday, when he fled in the company of Kyung-Soon Kim, who is believed to be his birth mother.

There was more. The article ran all the way down the page. Roni read the whole thing, every word, about ten times, each time pausing to admire the photo of herself at the bottom of the column and the caption beneath it:

"Article written by P. Q. Delicata, a student at Bloodwater High School. Ms. Delicata plans to be an investigative reporter."

The phone rang. Roni ignored it. Part of her punishment for the unauthorized trip to St. Paul was no phone and no computer for one solid week.

A few seconds later, Nick called to her.

"Roni! That was Darwin, from the garage."

"What did he want?" Roni asked, following her mother's voice into the kitchen.

"He wants to know when you and Brian can get started."

"Started doing what?"

"He said you and Brian agreed to help him clean up his back lot."

"Oh." Roni's shoulders sagged. "Did you tell him I'm grounded?"

Nick laughed. "I told him you'd be over later this morning."

"But I'm *grounded*."

"For this, I can make an exception," said Nick.

After six hours of hard labor, Roni and Brian had barely made a dent in the chaos of Darwin Dipstick's junkyard. As near as Roni could tell, whenever Darwin found himself with a possibly useful piece of automotive technology—a slightly bent wheel rim, for example—he would simply fling it out his back door and let the weeds grow up around it.

She bent over—for the thousandth time that day—and picked up something that looked like a transparent amber helmet.

"What's *this*?" she asked Brian, who was dragging a rusty fender from one weedy heap to a pile against the south fence.

"Looks like a light bubble off a tow truck," Brian said. "Throw it in the miscellaneous pile." He pointed at one of the larger piles they had created.

"How much more do you think we have to do?"

"You're the one who told Darwin we'd clean up his yard if he drove us up to St. Paul."

"I guess I didn't make such a good deal." She sat down on a stack of tires and watched Brian work for a few minutes. When he gave her an accusing look, she said, "Hey, you found your mom and brother. I didn't get squat out of this deal."

"You got an article published," he said, "and the satisfaction of seeing justice done."

"Justice schmustice! I'd rather have the hundred thousand dollars. But your stupid brother had to go and disappear on us."

"At least the Kays finally know what happened to their daughter. And they were happy to hear that their grandson was alive and well."

"Yeah, but there was no reward, because we couldn't actually give them their grandson!"

"We couldn't have turned him in anyway. It wouldn't have been right."

"I know." Roni sighed.

"And now that the Kays know that Billy is with his biological mom, they've canceled the reward. Louella Doblemun probably won't try to hunt him down again since Lance is in jail and there's no money to be had."

Roni picked up a rusty bolt and tossed it in the direction of the miscellaneous pile. "I still think she should have been arrested, too."

"Problem is, she didn't actually do anything illegal."

"A mere technicality."

"At least you're getting your Vespa fixed," Brian said.

"Yeah, but my mom says I can't use it for a month."

"I'm grounded, too. Except for doing this." He gestured at the junkyard surrounding them.

"It's like prison labor," Roni said. "We solve a horrendous crime and we're the ones doing hard labor. It's not fair."

"It never is," Brian said.

Brian felt half dead by the time he got home and fell into the chair in front of his computer. He was stinky and sweaty and covered with scratches. He decided to check his e-mail before he took a shower.

A new message popped up with the subject line "Hey, bro."

> I hacked your e-mail address off the Bloodwater High website. Better tell your webmaster to crank up the security! You never know who's gonna come looking for you. :-)
>
> Sorry we had to bug out on you, but if we'd stayed, Mom would have got in big trouble, and I might have ended up living with the Dobble-monster.
>
> Can't say where we are, but it's someplace safe. I'll come back sometime to see you, I promise. Maybe we can go visit old Lance in jail. lol.
>
> Later, bro,
> Billy

Brian reached out and touched his hand to the screen. One day he would see Billy and Kyung-Soon again.

He looked at the photos taped to the wall behind his computer. Brian Bain, winning the paper-airplane contest. Bryce Doblemun, the age-progressed image from the missing-kids website. And a photo of Billy Kim sailing down a ramp at some skateboard park, long hair flying, earring glinting in the sun—a photo Brian had found displayed on Kyung-Soon's night table. He knew that she had left it behind for him.

In that moment, he felt incredibly lucky. Some kids had only one family. He had two families—even if one of them was on the run.

He heard the slam of a car door, then the sound of the doorbell. For a moment, he allowed himself to think it might be Kyung-Soon and Billy dropping by for a visit—even though he knew they were far, far away. He heard his dad's voice and a woman's voice. Then his dad called out to him.

"Brian! Could you come down here, son?"

Brian ran downstairs and out to the front door, where he was greeted by an excited yelp.

"You have a visitor," his dad said as a small dog launched himself toward Brian's chest. Sniffer! Brian caught the dog in his arms. Jack and Theresa Hanke, who were standing at the bottom of the steps, laughed as Sniffer tried to lick the skin off Brian's face.

"After you two came to visit, ol' Sniffer just wasn't himself," said Mr. Hanke.

"He whined all night long," Mrs. Hanke added. "We were thinking he might be happier living with you, if you want him."

"*Want* him?" Brian said. Then he looked at his dad and his voice dropped. "But you're allergic."

Mr. Bain shrugged and said, "I could take some allergy medicine. You know, respiratory allergies are merely the body's attempts to deal with environmental irritants found in airborne particles such as—"

"Dad!" Brian said, stopping the flow of words. "Seriously! I can keep him?"

"Yes, son, Sniffer can come live with us."

PETE HAUTMAN is the author of several novels for young adults, including *Rash*, *Invisible*, and *Godless*, for which he won the 2004 National Book Award. Several of his books have received ALA Best Book for Young Adults citations.

MARY LOGUE has written several adult mysteries. Her first teen novel, *Dancing with an Alien*, was an ALA Best Book for Young Adults, a Quick Pick for Reluctant Readers, and a New York Public Library Book for the Teen Age.

Both Pete and Mary live in Golden Valley, Minnesota.

You can visit them both at

www.petehautman.com

FOLLOW ALL THE ADVENTURES OF RONI AND BRIAN IN THE EDGAR-NOMINATED BLOODWATER MYSTERIES!

"Effectively mixing suspense and humor, the authors have created interactions between complete opposites that are great fun."

—*School Library Journal* for *Snatched*

"Give this solid marks for plotting and characterization, as well as for suspense." —*Booklist* for *Snatched*

"Written with wit and style . . . enjoy this satisfying page-turner." —*Booklist* for *Skullduggery*